THE KING OF FOOTBALL

PELÉ

A COMPLETE BIOGRAPHY

PUSHKAR KUMAR

PRABHAT
PRAKASHAN

Published by
PRABHAT PRAKASHAN
4/19 Asaf Ali Road,
New Delhi-110 002 (INDIA)
e-mail: prabhatbooks@gmail.com

ISBN 978-93-5521-753-0
PELÉ: A COMPLETE BIOGRAPHY
by Pushkar Kumar

Edition
First, 2023

Price
₹ 250 (Rupees Two Hundred Fifty Only)

Printed at
Sanjay Printers, Sahibabad

To the Captain of 2022 FIFA World Cup Winner Argentina football team, 'Lionel Messi'.

Author's Note

In the 1970s, when the great soccer player Pelé arrived in the United States to play for the New York Cosmos in the North American Soccer League. The American newspaper readers and television viewers were told that he was a world-famous celebrity.

Since football was not given much importance as a sport in America at that time, this great Brazilian player also decided to return from retirement and play. The self-centred Americans could not believe that the most successful football player had come to play in their country.

But the world did not doubt Pelé's greatness. American sports fans could not understand how Pelé had fascinated the world. From South to Central America, Europe, and Africa, there has been a tremendous craze for football. While football is the most popular sport in most countries of the world, the game is also inextricably linked with the cultures of all those countries.

Pelé's popularity as the best player in the world, and that too as the best player of all time, had transcended borders and spread throughout the world. For all the football loving countries on earth, Pelé had become a God-like figure. The President of America may be the most powerful man in the world, but Pelé was also getting recognition throughout the world.

Football has been particularly popular among the poor around the world. It does not require any fancy equipments to play, and people living in backward or remote areas can easily play it with a ball. If they cannot find a ball, they can play the game by using an object that is similar to a ball.

Pelé had become such a sensational player that even people who did not understand the game of football properly or were not even interested in the game of football, were fascinated by him. His skills impressed people. It did not matter that Pelé belonged to the black population.

Over the decades, from representing his country as a teenager at the 1958 World Cup to the following years, Pelé's reputation grew and so did his stature. He is the only player in the history of football to score 1000 goals. This is such a magical figure that he was considered a charismatic player like a magician.

Not only that, when Pelé would come in front of the people of Brazil and the rest of the world, he would charm everyone with his graciousness and vivacity. He was constantly seen giving autographs. He laughed heartily when he won and accepted defeat with humility. He presented himself to the world as a great human being and a great sportsman.

Pelé's original name is Edson Arantes do Nascimento. The world does not know him by such a long and complex name. He only uses this name to sign legal documents. In his youth, he was called Pelé and he became famous by this name all over the world.

Brazil not only prides upon Pelé who has brought glory to the country through their beloved game but also considers him equal to a national heritage.

There was a time when Pelé became the richest player in the world through his earnings from the game. But like many other contemporary players of his time, people took advantage of his civility and he lost his hard-earned money. He played his last match for Brazil in 1971. However, even after that, he remained a popular player and the nation's pride.

From his teens to his thirties, Pelé's career developed through major matches he played for the national team and the Brazilian club team. Several times he was given tempting offers by wealthy clubs from other countries to join them, but Pelé remained loyal to his Santos club, rejecting such temptations.

Pelé retired from the sport in the mid-1970s when he felt his pace had slowed down. At that time, he was persuaded to play for an American team. It was a great achievement for the New York Cosmos that they were able to bring a great player like Pelé back from retirement. Pelé was offered a hefty sum to play, but the money didn't matter much to him. He had rejected tempting monetary offers earlier, too. He wanted to increase the popularity of football in the richest country in the world.

At the time of retirement, Pelé had scored 1283 goals. This is a unique and extraordinary record. The greatness of Pelé can be assessed from this data.

Pelé died at the age of 82 on December 29, 2022 after suffering from colon cancer and kidney problems for a year.

The multifaceted life of Pelé is portrayed in this book.

–Pushkar Kumar

Contents

Initial Stage

When Pelé was young, he was greatly influenced and inspired by his father who played football. The game of football was infused with the soil of his native land and his father was an accomplished football player.

In his childhood, Pelé would keenly watch his father play football. Whenever he had a chance to watch his father play for his club team, he was awestruck by his father's passion and energy.

It is true that the person who trained Pelé in football tricks during his childhood was present in his house only. This is how Edson Arantes do Nascimento was introduced to football and started learning the game.

His father Dondinho and mother Dona Celeste, who did not like football, could not afford to buy football-related equipment for their son due to their poverty, but Pelé found a way.

The eldest son of the family was born on October 23, 1940, in the Brazilian community of Três Corações, Brazil. Três Corações literally means 'Three Hearts'. Três Corações is located in the province of Minas Gerais and the boy, who would later be called Pelé, was born in poverty.

Despite Dondinho's hard work and efforts, the family remained poor. Dona Celeste was from Três Corações and had met Pelé's father Dondinho when he was posted there for military service. Dona Celeste was just 15 when she got married and at the age of 16, she gave birth to Pelé.

For many years, the family continued to face the challenge of making both ends meet. So, there was no question about buying shoes or balls to play football. Such things were deemed luxury.

The boys in the local communities were obsessed with the country's most popular sport and wanted to play football at any cost. Dondinho stuffed an old sock with scraps of cloth and made it into a made, which was enough to satisfy the five-year-old Pelé.

Dondinho was passionately devoted to football and was very talented. He was a popular player and played for the city club. But the team did not have enough money and could only afford to pay small sums to its players.

Despite this, Dondinho was considered a player of great potential and in 1942, when Pelé was two years old, Dondinho was selected by the Atlético Mineiro club to play in the provincial capital. It was a golden opportunity through which Dondinho was not only going to get a chance to showcase his talent in the big arena but would also get better remuneration.

But destiny played a cruel joke on him. A collision with a player from the rival team during his first match for his new club ruined Dondinho's career. Dondinho suffered a knee injury and as a result, was unable to play.

The new team paid for Dondinho's return fare and sent him back to Três Corações.

At that time, reliable surgery for such knee injuries was still in its infancy, and Dondinho did not believe in such surgery. He put aside the intention of operation and left the knee in the injured condition and it did not get cured. After that incident, he lost his momentum. However, he did not give up trying to play.

Because of this incident, Pelé's mother Dona Celeste began to dislike football. She started calling this game 'silly'. Her husband's love for football remained unwavering as before, but his earning capacity continued to decline—it was not possible to earn particularly through football.

The next two years were very difficult. Then Dondinho received a new offer. The offer came from a football team called FC Bauru. It came with an opportunity for a civil service job. The family shifted to another location.

This time it seemed that the family was about to get rid of the troubles. But once again Dondinho was struck with bad luck. The ownership of the team changed. Dondinho was kept on the team, but the provision for the civil service job was ended whereas Dondinho had accepted the offer because of the offer of the job.

The family was getting bigger. Pelé's brother Zoca and sister Maria Lucia had already been born. Pelé's maternal Uncle Jorge and grandmother Emosina were also part of the family.

They had gone to live in a strange city with the hope of finding better means of livelihood, but destiny did not favour them. Dondinho faced severe mental pressure now.

"And we were excited," Pelé said. "But when I grew up, I understood the meaning of poverty. Poverty is a curse, which makes the mind gloomy, crushes the soul and poisons one's life. There was an environment of love in that small house and difficulties were fought only with the help of love."

As seen in all families, Pelé's mindset was deeply influenced by the family atmosphere during his childhood. After the family shifted to Bauru, Pelé started getting ample opportunities to play with the children in the neighbourhood.

Later, Pelé reflected on the poverty he experienced during his childhood. He said that the locality where his family lived was inhabited by only poor people. Everyone faced scarcity. Since the economic plight of those families was similar, they did not harbour feelings of jealousy towards each other. None of the families had the means of luxury.

Later, when Pelé became rich, he recalled the difficult days of his childhood and described the agonies of poverty.

"There was such poverty that we used to worry about how we would light the stove if there was no money for fuel?" He said, "There was such poverty that we would hesitate to put wood in the stove. Poverty means losing self-respect and self-confidence. There is a fear of poverty. There is no fear of death because it is sure to come. It is the fear of being alive. It is a terrifying fear."

There were many children in his neighbourhood and all used to play in the open space. People of different communities live in Brazil. That was why white and black children and children of mixed colour lived in that locality. Everyone played together and there was no discrimination among them.

The colour of Pelé's skin was black, but many people in Brazil are of mixed race. The children used to play circus games. They would play different games in the backyard of Pelé's house.

Pelé later said that he would be busy playing with the children from morning till evening. Then the kids got drawn to football. As Pelé recalls the first ball was made with the help of an old sock. Pieces of old newspaper were inserted inside it and it was tied with a rope to give it a shape of a ball.

Pelé said, "As we became more skilled, and grew older, we started stuffing more junk inside the socks to make bigger balls." "Many times, we used to make balls of socks without letting the owner of the socks know about it or stuff other people's clothes inside them. We thought it appropriate to take such steps to fulfill our needs. A man can walk without socks, but a child needs a ball to play."

When Pelé started playing football, he started enjoying the game a lot. But he did not think about making a career out of this game. He wanted to become a pilot. He never thought of becoming a professional football player. Football was the national game of the country. This game beat in the hearts of the citizens of Brazil.

Later, when Pelé became a national hero, he recalled the early part of his life and said that his approach to the game during those childhood years could be summed up in these philosophical words—"If it rolls, kick it. If it doesn't roll, kick it and force it to roll. If hitting is a problem because of the size, then hit a smaller ball."

With its area and population, Brazil is the largest country in South America. It is the fifth largest country in the world. Its border extends over 3.3 million square miles. It was a sparsely populated country when Pelé was born, but now it has a population of about 200 million.

The Portuguese conquered Brazil during the Age of Exploration and ruled the tropical country from 1500 to 1815. Brazil gained full independence in 1822. But whereas the language of most countries in the continent is Spanish, the language of Brazil is Portuguese.

Brazil wood trees are found in abundance on its beaches and the country was named after it. These trees also have played a role in the country's wealth. This country receives abundant rainfall. The climate here is hot and humid. Part of the Amazon rainforest falls in Brazil. The residents of Brazil are religious by nature and Roman Catholicism is prevalent here.

When it comes to sports, the sports such as auto racing, basketball and volleyball are seen to be popular in Brazil. But, the craze people have for football, is unrivalled compared to other sports. This craze was seen even during Pelé's time.

Pelé's achievements further strengthened Brazilians' love for football, and the country set a record by winning the World Cup five times. The credit for this record is also given to Pelé.

But the boy who kicked a ball made out of a sock was very different from the miraculous football player who had achieved extraordinary feats. That was the future; the little boy was playing with the ball made of socks only to amuse himself.

In childhood, Edson was called 'Diko' by his father, but only family members know this name. No one outside the family called him by this name.

At the age of 10, when Edson was playing with his friends, he got a new name. Pelé's childhood, career, and achievements in football are all linked to the mystery of his name 'Pelé', a name that he got by chance. It is believed that his teammates started calling him Pelé while playing in the streets, but none of his teammates has taken credit for this name to date.

The strangest part is that there is no personal image or any quality of him as a player attached to this nomenclature. It is not even an official word in the Portuguese language. This unique and glorious name sprung up suddenly one day and then endured.

"I don't know how I got that name or who first started calling me by that name!" Pelé said. "The name has no meaning in Portuguese, nor is the word used in any other language."

Many years after he was given this name, Pelé returned to Bauru and met old friends and requested them to tell him whatever they remembered about the name given to him. But his friends did not remember anything.

Pelé said, "They did not know anything about its origin or of its usage. All they said was that one day the name suddenly appeared and everyone started liking the name even though no one knew its meaning."

However, Pelé certainly invented a story based on speculation about his name. The following story gives an idea about how he might have got the new name 'Pelé'. There was a goalkeeper named Bilé on his father's club team. As a child, Pelé used to watch his father and Bilé play. It is possible that when Pelé defended a goal brilliantly, the players called him 'little Bilé' which might have changed to Pelé later.

Pelé said, "Perhaps I changed my name on my own as my Uncle Jorge told me, or maybe I was so named because of a mistake in my pronunciation." This argument put forth by Pelé also does not seem credible since people started calling him by this name only after many years.

It could also be that because he was a unique player, friends started calling him Pelé. He is as unique a player as this name. Obviously, at that time, no one imagined that this boy named Pelé would one day become famous all over the world and the whole world would rave about his skills. Now if other children in Brazil are also named Pelé, then it is because of the inspiration that they take from Pelé's success.

An interesting fact is that when initially his teammates started calling him Pelé, he found it quite insulting. He also fought with his friends about it, but he would lose the fight, and eventually, he gave up trying to change the perception of the people. If his punches had been more powerful in his childhood and he could beat up his friends well, then perhaps the world would have known the best football player as 'Edson' or people would have simply called him 'Ed'.

Pelé started going to school with the children he played with on the streets. But he did not like sitting in the classroom. The classroom seemed like a prison to him compared to the freedom he felt while playing outside.

It was not as if he did not understand what the teacher taught, but he could not concentrate on his studies and he regretted it in the later years of his life.

While the teachers tried to teach him maths, geography and social science, his mind was fixed on only one subject—football. He used to dream of playing football even during classes at his school.

Pelé first set the goal of becoming a pilot, but it did not take him long to change this goal. Pelé must have decided to become a pilot after seeing the thrill associated with the life of a pilot.

Whenever he had time, he would go to the local aero club. As he watched the pilots, he would dream of wearing dark glasses and a leather jacket like them. He wanted to become a pilot in the future and wear nice outfits.

One day, Pelé and his friends were peeping through the window of the aero club. They saw people taking out the body of a pilot from inside a crashed glider. After that incident, Pelé had nightmares during his sleep for several days and he gave up the intention of becoming a pilot forever.

Pelé felt bored at school and did not like the teachers. When he completed the fourth grade, he told his family that he wanted to give up his studies in order to work. His family allowed him to do so. Sometimes he would brainstorm plans with his friends to earn money.

When Pelé had not formally left school, he would leave aside his homework and work as a shoe polisher. He would go to the neighbouring houses for this work. His mother had forbidden him to go far away from home, but he still went far.

Executing the first plan to earn together with his friends, Pelé started stealing peanuts from a warehouse and selling them. With the money earned in this way, Pelé and his friends bought the clothes, except for shoes, essential for playing football.

Although he went on stealing for a few days, Pelé soon realized that in the future he could be caught, jailed, and declared a criminal. He soon abandoned this means of earning.

Then, Pelé started collecting soccer cards and kept them in albums. Trading those cards, he bought a ball. Later, Pelé began working as an assistant to a cobbler. He received a little over two dollars a month, which was a reasonable amount.

Pelé regularly played football with his friends. But due to poverty, he had to play football barefoot. Pelé and his teammates did not have the financial means to buy the shoes needed for the game. The name of his team was *Sajember Seven*, but everyone called them 'Shoeless Players'.

When Pelé turned ten, his father recognized his talent and began to mentor him. He also started taking his son along with him to the playground. His father started training young Pelé the tricks of the game. He taught his son the skill of using both feet on the ground.

The mayor's office of Bauru was sponsoring a local football tournament and Pelé wanted to participate with his teammates.

The father of three players promised to provide shoes to all the players on the team, but in return, he wanted to take on the role of the team's coach. He had not bought those shoes, rather he had asked for old shoes from another team. It didn't matter to Pelé and his teammates—their wildest desire was getting fulfilled.

The team was renamed 'Little America'. Twelve-year-old Pelé was the youngest player on this team. Playing in front of 5,000 spectators, Pelé scored the winning goal and took hold of the 'Junior Victory Cup'. Pelé and his teammates felt as though they had won the World Cup.

That day of victory was one of the most memorable days in Pelé's life. Each member of the team was given a cash prize. The value of 36 cruzeiros was not much, but all the players on the team handed over their share of the money to Pelé, who had played an extraordinary game.

Dona Celeste was not present on the field and had never seen her son play. She told Pelé to divide the prize money among all the players. Pelé did just that. However, monetary reward seemed insignificant to Pelé that day.

"Of all the memories I have of that glorious day, I will never forget two things," Pelé said. "The crowd kept shouting my name—'Pelé-Pelé', and I didn't mind being called by that name for the first time. Then as soon as the match was over, my father wrapped me in his arms and said—You played a great game."

This match proved to be a turning point in Pelé's life. His extraordinary performance in a well-organized tournament was witnessed by a large number of people. The audience also included people who had influence in the world of football. They had seen the astonishing game of a talented teenager with their own eyes.

Waldemar de Brito was a respected figure in the world of football, who had been on the national scene for many years. He had participated in the 1934 World Cup as a player on the Brazilian team and also had coached the Bauru team for which Dondinho was selected.

Brito had personally seen Pelé play, and Pelé's father did not need to recommend his son. Pelé was not even twelve-years-old, but Brito recognized his talent well enough—"I could not believe my eyes how such a young boy could exhibit such exquisite details. Pelé moved with the ball with ease dodging rivals," said Brito.

There is a certain risk involved in training teenagers. At the time, no one can say with certainty whether that teenager will remain completely devoted to the game in the future as well. Apart from this, the mental and physical development of the teenager is also an important aspect, which needs to be paid attention. It is also important to know whether the teenager is really talented or not. Is he merely perceived as a genius because he is playing against his average friends and winning?

Brito was convinced that Pelé had an innate talent. His charisma was not going to fade after his teenage, rather he would also perform well in adulthood. There was a certain rare quality to the teenage Pelé's style. Looking at the manner in which he won the tournament and the maturity he displayed, one could be sure about his future.

"I can honestly say that over the years I have been watching teenage football players play. I saw potential in many of those teenagers, but no one else impressed me the way Pelé's game impressed me." Brito said.

Brito said, "And I could not believe that he was only a twelve-year-old boy. Seeing his tricks, I was reminded of the great players of my time. I compared myself with him. At his age, I was not able to play with such skill. He was way ahead of me in that sense."

Brito formed a junior Bauru club with Pelé at centre. Now, there was no dearth of shoes and Pelé started playing football with full passion.

However, Brito wanted to move to the big city and returned to his hometown of São Paulo to train professional footballers. Pelé was offered to play with a club team called Radium. Despite being a non-professional player on this team, Pelé scored 40 goals. People were stunned when they saw Pelé playing. They thought that this boy was going to do wonders in the future.

Along with learning the nuances of the game, Pelé also sold meat pies to passengers at the railway station. After he had sold meat pies several times, his patrons discovered a discrepancy in the accounts. The patrons assumed that the impoverished Pelé must have eaten the meat pies himself while Pelé argued that someone had stolen his meat pies. Pelé returned to school and completed his eighth-grade education.

Pelé was 15 when Brito approached him again. He had kept an eye on Pelé's progress even from afar. He found Pelé looking fitter than before and youthful. Now Brito wanted to take Pelé to the Brazilian national team.

Brito wanted to take Pelé away from his home town. He wanted to sign Pelé with the leading Santos club. Pelé's mother, Dona Celeste, did not like the idea. She didn't want to let her son out of her sight. She knew that Brito wanted their son to join the world of professional football players and Dona did not like the professional world of football at all.

Santos was located on the coast, 300 miles from São Paulo. Pelé's mother initially did not allow her son to go there.

Due to Brito's efforts, the president of the Santos club came over to meet Pelé's parents and assured them that Pelé would be well taken care of and safe given his young age. Not only that but

Pelé would also be given an attractive remuneration. Dona Celeste cried and reluctantly blessed her son to go.

Dona Celeste knew that Pelé had not proved to be a brilliant student and that he would not have the opportunity to advance in the world of white people. She didn't want her son to be a cobbler's assistant all his life.

Dona Celeste said, "You are still a little boy in my eyes. But everyone thinks that you have grown up. You have never been able to concentrate on your studies and I do not want you to work as a cobbler for the rest of your life."

The deal was done. Dondinho and Pelé boarded the train and left for Santos. Pelé's family was not rich enough to own a car. Pelé had not travelled anywhere before. So, traveling by train was a new experience for him. When the train started, he felt nervous with the excitement of entering a new world. He started having cramps in his stomach. He told his father that he wanted to get down from the train. His father calmed him down. The distance from Bauru to Santos was 312 miles.

As soon as they arrived at Santos, Brito took Pelé and his father to the stadium, where football practice was in progress. At the end of practice, Pelé was introduced to the new coach and new environment.

Brito had already spoken about Pelé's skills and abilities. He told Santos club representatives, "This boy is going to be the greatest football player in the world."

The name of the coach was Luis Alonso also known as Lula. Luis said to Pelé, "So you are the famous Pelé." Everyone already knew Pelé because of Brito's appreciation.

When Pelé was introduced to the players, Dondinho found that all of them were older than Pelé. Hiding his uneasiness, he politely said that he himself wanted to take care of his son's safety. He felt that the club's older players would not be able to accept Pelé easily and would deliberately try to injure him while playing.

But Dondinho's fears were proved wrong. The players of the team warmly welcomed Pelé and everyone started treating him like a younger brother.

Pelé was a centre-forward player and had a central position. This was a space where a strong player displaying creativity could create chances for a goal.

Initially, Pelé was homesick. He was also nervous playing alongside players much older than himself. He was thin and weighed 130 pounds. He looked weak compared to other players. Although he was agile, he did not have enough strength to defend. Lula understood this aspect and understood that his young player could be badly injured by rival players. Hence, eating a full meal was made mandatory in Pelé's training programme.

Pelé had grown up in an environment of poverty and scarcity. When he started getting plenty of food, it was no less than a boon for him. He had not expected such hospitality. Although his diet was carefully selected and he was prevented from eating junk food he was allowed to become strong by eating aplenty. As he practised with the A team, he faced limited competition.

Though his team players loved him, they would ask him to bring coffee due to his young age. In later years, Pelé said that for a few days he had found a new name. Santos' players used to say—"Bring me coffee, kid, and don't waste gasoline." The players started calling him 'Gasoline'.

Despite being so passionate about football and being a part of a top-class team, Pelé became very homesick. One day he packed his stuff and quietly prepared to leave at five in the morning to board the train.

A team assistant named Big Saboo spotted him, and after much persuasion, Pelé gave up the idea to return home.

During his training period, Pelé played in several matches as a member of Santos' junior team and performed well. Satisfied with his performance, the club members decided to sign a contract to keep him on the team permanently. But because of Pelé's age, signing such a contract was not valid.

After consulting legal experts, a contract was signed on April 8, 1956, stipulating a monthly remuneration of 1,000 cruzeiros for Pelé. The contract tied Pelé to the club for eighteen months.

In the first half of 1957, though Pelé was taking part in games regularly and scoring goals every now and then, his fame was limited to the local level.

For the first time in June 1957, Pelé had the opportunity to showcase his talent at the national level. A tournament was going to be held in Rio de Janeiro between four European clubs and four Brazilian clubs. A Brazilian team was being formed consisting of players from Santos and Rio's Vasco da Gama club. Pelé was selected to play as a centre-forward in the team.

Thus, for the first time in his life, Pelé had the opportunity to visit Rio de Janeiro, which was 300 miles from Santos. Once there, Pelé realized that the city was bigger than Santos. The coach took him straight to the Vasco Stadium in São Januário, where after a day's practice, they were put up in dormitories.

❑

Santos to Sweden

Pelé was going to play in the Maracanã stadium for the first time and was very excited about it. He knew this stadium from the time of the 1950 World Cup. This stadium was built for competitions and was the largest stadium in the world.

He first participated in the practice session in this stadium. The first match was played by the Santos/Vasco All-Stars against the Belenenses team from Portugal. The stadium was packed with spectators. There was a spectacular fireworks display before the start of the game. Pelé scored three goals in this match.

Pelé scored three goals using different styles and all the spectators present there were stunned by his ability.

Pelé also scored in the other two matches of the tournament, against Flamengo and São Paulo. His performance impressed the selectors and he was invited to be a part of the national team.

The Brazil against Argentina match was held at the Maracanã Stadium. Pelé came on the field in the second half. He was wearing the number 10 jersey. At that time, Argentina was leading by 1–0. Moments later Pelé scored. Argentina won the match 2–1.

The second match against Argentina was held in São Paulo, in which Pelé took the field with the starting line-up for the first time. Pelé scored after 18 minutes and the second goal was scored by his teammate Mazzola. Brazil won the match by 2–0.

Pelé chose the number 10 jersey for himself while playing throughout the season with Santos. He scored seventeen goals, which was the highest number of goals, in matches of the São Paulo State Championship.

Due to training and an adequate diet, Pelé began to experience positive changes in his personality. In a span of six months, his muscles had become stronger than before.

Pelé worked hard during practice. He found his left leg weaker than his right leg, so he would do exercises to strengthen it. Along with this, he developed the skill of heading by hitting the ball that hung with the help of a rope.

The Santos club had its own gym, where Pelé trained in karate for a year. Through karate, he learned how to get up safely after falling on the ground. After that, he took training in Judo. Practising Judo-Karate helped him a lot in increasing his balance and concentration. In this way, when an opponent player used to push him in the field, he could defend himself with determination.

Pelé was the youngest player among all the players to play in the league. During that time, Pelé closely observed the skills of experienced players like Zizinho. Zizinho had participated in the 1950 World Cup and was now playing for São Paulo in the league tournament.

In one such match in November 1957, a fine performance from Zizinho helped São Paulo win by 6–2. Pelé was thrilled to have the opportunity to play amid such a great player as Zizinho. São Paulo won the regional championship that year with the help of Zizinho's stellar performance.

Pelé had been a fan of Zizinho right from the beginning. Seeing his fitness, he was asked to play in the 1958 World Cup, but he declined. Perhaps he knew that he was past his prime. He is remembered as one of the great Brazilian players who was not destined to win a World Cup.

Zizinho may have defeated Santos' team by a margin of 6–2, but he later praised Pelé's performance – "He fought like a true warrior throughout the match. I found his technique very impressive. I knew that he was going to go ahead and I was not wrong in believing so."

Many years later, Pelé told Zizinho that he considered him his role model. Zizinho wrote back to him—"Great King Pelé, the best player of this century, if I was like a useful mirror at the beginning of your career, then be sure to know that I am proud to know that."

In the first half of 1958, a sense of excitement had naturally pervaded the minds of the club's players. The World Cup was going to be held that year. All the players were trying extra hard to impress the national team selectors with their best performance.

Pelé's father, Dondinho, received information that Pelé was going to be selected for the national team, but he was not entirely sure of the information. He telephoned Bauru to tell Pelé what he had heard on the radio and that he could not say with certainty whether the name of Telê, who played for the national team for Fluminense, had been mentioned or it was Pelé's.

"I think you've been selected to the team, son," his father told Pelé emotionally.

Pelé began enquiring with the Santos club officials. Club president Athiê Jorge Coury told him, "Kid, you've been selected."

Vicente Feola was given the responsibility of taking the Brazilian players to Sweden. Feola prepared the final list of players and on the basis of that list, the players could board the plane.

The system of selection was so complicated that sometimes the list was changed at the last minute even after the players were called. Naturally, that increased the nervousness of all the players during this process.

All the players had to appear before the head of the Brazilian delegation, Paulo Machado de Carvalho. He announced the names of the selected players, including Pelé. But Luizinho, a popular player of the Corinthian club, was not selected.

The coach's decision used to be considered final. But the decision not to include Luizinho in the team sparked such a strong backlash that a practice match was organized in Pakenbu to allow Luizinho to prove his merit.

Luizinho did not perform well in this match. However, Pelé injured his knee during this match.

Following the injury, team doctor Hilton Gosling and physiotherapist Mário Américo began treating Pelé. Doctor Gosling encouraged Pelé telling him that there was nothing much to worry about. Ice was placed on the area that was swollen due to injury.

Mário Américo reassured Pelé, saying, "You will be absolutely fine." Whereas Pelé was apprehensive about whether he would get a chance to participate in the World Cup or not. After struggling a lot, Dr. Gosling decided to keep Pelé on the team.

On May 24, 1958, Pelé travelled by plane for the first time in his life and arrived in Lisbon after a twelve-hour flight as a member of the Brazilian team. The Brazilian team reached Rome after a three-hour flight from Lisbon.

The team was arranged to stay at the Hotel Universo in Rome. In preparation for the World Cup, Brazil's sports authorities had arranged two friendly warm-up matches with Italian clubs.

The first match was to be held in Florence with the Fiorentina club. Prior to the match, Pelé's knee was inspected and he was not allowed to participate in the match due to his injury. In fact, Dr. Gosling was concerned that it would take more than a month for Pelé's knee to heal. But he did not express his concern.

Pelé became very anxious. He felt that he might be deprived of playing in the World Cup due to his injury. Paulo Machado had decided to take a decision in this regard only on the basis of the doctor's opinion. Jose de Almeida, director of the national team, had demanded Pelé's return to Brazil. However, Pelé was not informed of this demand.

The doctor warned Pelé that if he really wanted to play at the World Cup in Sweden, he needed to fully cooperate with the painful treatment process for his knee.

Pelé had no choice. He started with the treatment. Towels soaked in hot water were placed on his knee, which was a very painful process.

The second practice match was played with the International Club in Milan. Pelé was not in a condition to play this match either.

On June 2, 1958, the Brazilian team reached Gothenburg by air. The first match was to start six days later. Brazil was in Group 4 with Austria, England and the Soviet Union.

The Brazilian team was accommodated in a comfortable hotel at a place called Hindas. All the food and drinks were available in the hotel for the players.

Pelé was impressed by the natural beauty of Sweden. Sweden had many lakes and plenty of greenery. The people there were polite and courteous.

There was a feeling of friendship and camaraderie between the players of the Brazilian team. Everyone would laugh and joke with each other. They would train and practice regularly in order to play in the match.

From time to time, Pelé would go to Kiesberg Park in Gothenburg to hang out with his fellow players. He would go to the dance hall for entertainment. The players had become friends with the Swedish girls. Pelé would also go fishing sometimes. While fishing, Pelé liked the calm environment around. He would imagine his knee recovering and playing in a World Cup match.

Brazil's first match with Austria was held in Uddevalla. The doctor did not allow Pelé to participate in this match. Mazzola scored two goals and Nilton Santos scored one goal for Brazil, thus leading Brazil to victory.

Brazil's second match with England was held three days later in Gothenburg. Once again, Dr. Gosling did not allow Pelé to play. He said that Pelé's knee could be under pressure and that could lead to swelling.

In this match, England gave equal competition to Brazil. England players were fully prepared. Not a single goal had been scored during the entire match, which meant that the match had ended in a draw.

Blythe and Don Howe played brilliantly for England. Both of them kept the pressure on Brazilian player Didi. Although Vava once kicked the ball over the goal post, two of Mazzola's strikes were saved by England goalkeeper Colin McDonald.

The third and final match of the group stage was to be held with the Soviet Union. The result of this match could prove to be decisive for the Brazilian team. The Brazilian team was worried and not satisfied with its performance so far. The Soviet Union, on the other hand, had a strong team. On one hand, due to the Cold War, the dominance of the Soviet Union had remained unchanged, on the other, their team had won the gold medal during the 1952 Olympics held in Helsinki.

Like Brazil, the Soviet Union team had also defeated Austria and had a draw with England. That meant that the winner of the match between Brazil and the Soviet Union would also be the winner of the group.

At the time, Pelé was very disappointed as he had not been able to play in two matches. The day before the said match, Zito, the midfielder and Pelé's teammate at the Santos club, went to Pelé and said, "It seems that the decisive moment has come." Pelé said, "Is it about the most difficult match?" Zito said that Mazzola was not feeling well and believed that Pelé and Zito should get a chance to play.

Nascimento, a member of the Brazilian team, asked Pelé, "Are you ready? Feola is going to have you play in the match."

In the last training session, Pelé and Garrincha practiced as a part of the main team. This practice was to be held in the afternoon. But Feola learned that a journalist was working to pass information to the Soviet Union by keeping an eye on the Brazilian team. Feola decided at the last minute to hold the training session in the morning itself.

After breakfast, all the players were taken to the ground for training. Pelé knew that all eyes were going to be on him during the training session. Pelé had become alert and was eager to demonstrate his fitness.

Pelé entered the field and after initial hesitation started running and jumping as before. He no longer had any difficulty in bending his knee and his confidence got stronger.

Later, Paulo wrote about the experience that Feola came to him and said, "Thank God, the boy looks completely in his old form." Paulo asked, "Will he be able to play the match?" Feola said, "Of course, I have been waiting for this day." Doctor Gosling also gave his consent and said that Pelé's knee was cured.

However, there was still an obstacle in Pelé's way. To test the preparation of the players of the team, the psychiatrist of the team, Dr. João Carvalhaes, gave a test to all the players. During the test, they were asked to draw a sketch and answer questions. Based on these answers alone, Dr. Carvalhaes would recommend whether a player should be allowed to play in the match or not.

Doctor Carvalhaes rejected Pelé's name and remarked, "Pelé is immature. He doesn't have the mentality to fight." Carvalhaes had also rejected Garrincha's name and called him irresponsible.

Feola had full confidence in the competence of Pelé and Garrincha. He told the psychiatrist, "Your opinion might be right, but you don't know anything about football. If Pelé's knee is fine, nothing can stop him from playing."

As soon as Pelé's name was announced as a team member, curiosity about him increased a lot all around. Pelé was merely seventeen years old and he was the youngest among all the players in the tournament. The media started discussing him. Prior to that, all the attention of the media was focused on the players of the Soviet Union. The Soviet team featured world-class players, such as famed goalkeeper, Yashin and striker Simonyan.

When Pelé ran onto the pitch at Gothenburg's Nya Ullevi Stadium on 15 June, fifty thousand spectators were spellbound as they looked at the young black man who was the youngest player. Pelé was wearing the number 10 jersey.

Pelé looked at the Soviet Union players, who looked tall and strong. He thought to himself, "These people are tall, but even tall trees break and fall."

Before Pelé entered the field, Mário Américo had massaged his knee one last time and said, "Now you have to keep running, kid."

Naturally, Pelé was overcome with emotion when he stood up to sing the national anthem with his teammates. His dream of playing in the World Cup was coming true. He had taken pains and trained hard for this day; he had taken treatment for so many days to cure his knee injury. Today he was representing Brazil, a country that loved football. On one hand, Pelé was a little nervous due to such a huge responsibility, on the other hand, he was also trying to concentrate on the game.

As the whistle blew, the Brazilian players began to play with more energy and enthusiasm than in the previous two matches. Garrincha began to move forward, controlling the ball with his feet and taking advantage of weaknesses in the Soviet defence. Garrincha took aim and tossed the ball, but the ball bounced back after hitting the post. At that moment, Pelé involuntarily blurted—"Goal!" His teammate Didi reassured him, saying, "Calm down kid, we will surely score a goal. There is no need to panic."

The spectators were mesmerized by Brazil's extraordinary pace in the first few minutes of the game. Brazil had a chance to dominate the game early on. Didi tossed the ball to Vava in a desperate manner and Vava lofted the ball straight into the net. Only three minutes had passed and Brazil had scored the first goal. The Brazilian players were jubilant.

The pace of the game had slowed down a bit. Pelé still felt pain in his knee, but he tried to hide his pain. He was under pressure to maintain the lead and knew that even the slightest mistake could cost them the game. He tried to score twice but was unsuccessful. He realized that if he did not have knee pain, he could have easily succeeded in his efforts.

In the second half, the Soviet players launched a counter-attack, but the Brazilian players fought valiantly. Vava shattered the morale of the Soviet team by scoring another goal. Vava was hugged by his fellow players. In this way, Brazil was confirmed to play in the quarter-finals.

That night a celebratory banquet was organised. When Pelé reached his room after the banquet, he did an in-depth analysis of his performance in the match.

He was not happy with his performance. He felt that he could have done much better.

The same evening the Brazilian team learned that they were to play their next match against Wales. Wales had defeated Hungary by 2–1 in their group. People were surprised at the success of Wales. But the Wales team had giant players like John Charles, although Charles was ruled out of the match against Brazil due to injury.

The match was going to take place only two days later. Wales' goalkeeper Jack Kelsey was in excellent form and their team had a strong defensive line. Neither side could score a single goal in the first half.

Feola spoke at halftime to encourage the Brazilian players. In the second half, Pelé was passed the ball by Didi from behind.

Pelé controlled the ball with his feet and hit the target restraining an opponent player. In this way, the ball went inside the net.

It was Pelé's first goal in the World Cup and Brazil won the match due to this goal. Brazil needed to win the match against the Soviet Union as winning that match would put them at the top of their group. On the other hand, Brazil's match against Wales was also gravely important. A loss to Wales could have meant elimination from the tournament.

Pelé has described his goal against Wales as the most memorable goal of his life. Because of this goal, Pelé's faltering self-confidence was strengthened anew. Sports lovers around the world started recognizing him.

The Brazilian team reached Stockholm to play in the semi-finals. Brazil was to play against France in the semi-finals. France had trounced Northern Ireland by 4–0 in the quarter-finals.

The semi-finals saw a thrilling contest between France and Brazil and a total of seven goals were scored.

Vava scored a goal as soon as the match started. Then the French player Fontaine (who had scored a record thirteen goals during the tournament) scored a goal and made the scores of both teams equal. Before the end of the first half, Didi scored a goal using the long drive technique to give Brazil the lead. In the second half, Pelé created a sensation by scoring three consecutive goals at the 52nd, 64th, and 75th minutes. The charismatic performance of a seventeen-year-old left everyone spellbound.

Now, Brazil had completely dominated the match. Though, Roger Piantoni scored a late goal for France, Brazil won the match by 5–2 and advanced to the finals.

Brazil's robust performance in the semi-finals increased Brazil's popularity among football fans. The European teams focus more on defence. That is why the number of defenders in European teams is higher as compared to attackers. On the other hand, the aggressive game exhibited by the Brazilian players naturally created a frenzy among the spectators.

While most teams in the tournament played in a 4–4–2 formation, the Brazilian team played in a 4–2–4 formation. The Brazilians believed in attacking immediately as soon as they had control of the ball, and their four frontline players executed the attacks.

Garrincha led Brazil's attack. When he ran forward controlling the ball with his feet, the rival players could not stop him easily. The audience applauded and appreciated this skill of Garrincha.

It was famously said about Garrincha that, once the ball went to him, the rival players could not snatch the ball from him under any circumstances. Actually, the rival teams could not comprehend, in which direction Garrincha would move with the ball. Hence, other Brazilian players were able to handle the front aggressively.

But many times, due to such unique skills of Garrincha, even his teammates could not understand to whom he actually wanted to pass the ball.

Like Garrincha, Didi was also an outstanding player in the Brazil team and at the end of the World Cup, he was awarded the best player of the tournament award.

While Garrincha and Pelé were younger players on the team, Didi was older and more adept at planning. In the field, he used to trick the opponent players badly and confuse them. When his own teammates would get confused, he would shout, "Not you stupid, I want to confuse the opposing team."

Pelé found that the players of all the teams participating in the World Cup were white. Expressing his surprise to one of his team members, he said—"It is so strange that there are black players only in the Brazilian team."

On the morning of June 29, 1958, a strong wind blew in Stockholm, and clouds gathered in the sky. The final match was to be held on that day. Everyone said that the Swedish team would benefit from that weather.

On the other hand, the Brazilian players were used to playing in the rain and would not have trouble playing in wet weather.

Sweden's players also wore yellow jerseys, so the colour of the Brazilian team's jersey was changed to blue. Some people in the Brazilian camp said that changing the colour of the jersey was not a good omen. But Dr. Paulo, the head of the Brazilian team, refuted the claims saying that the blue colour would prove to be auspicious for Brazil because it was the colour of Nossa Senhora de Piedade, Brazil's favourite saint. Not only that, this colour had proved to be auspicious for the team earlier as well. Wearing jerseys of this colour, the Brazilian team had won the semi-finals in the 1950 World Cup and entered the final.

Djalma Santos was selected to play in place of De Sordi in the Brazilian team. That was the only change made to the team. Some people speculated that Feola had denied De Sordi a chance to play in the final despite his superior performance and given this opportunity to Djalma Santos.

In fact, De Sordi was not well. The night before the final, Sordi had not slept well and he also had pain in one of his legs. He told Dr. Gosling about his pain and it was then decided to field Djalma Santos in his place.

A total of 49,737 spectators were present in the stadium that day. Though, most of the spectators were Swedish and supported their home team, they were also polite and courteous and applauded the excellent performance of both teams.

As the players of both teams lined up to sing the national anthem, Pelé visualized his father, Dondinho, sitting at home listening to the radio and feeling a mixture of trepidation and pride. Pelé wanted to make his father proud.

Sweden started the game very well and the centre-forward Liedholm scored a goal after just four minutes. The whole stadium erupted with noise. The spectators applauded the players of their team by waving their caps.

This was the first time in the tournament that the Brazilian players felt under pressure. Didi, Vava, and Pelé encouraged their teammates and motivated them to fight harder.

Garrincha regained control of the ball and Vava levelled the score by striking a goal. After a while, Garrincha again passed the ball to Vava as before and Vava took advantage of the opportunity to score the second goal. In this way, Brazil took the lead of 2–1 in the first half.

In the second half, the Brazilian players displayed a slower pace and attack. Eleven minutes later, Pelé scored a goal. The score was 3–1. Pelé shouted to Nilton Santos to cross a log centre. As soon as the ball reached him, he stopped it with the help of his chest. To stop him, rival player Gustavsson came close to him. Pelé easily dodged him to score the goal.

Pelé later described it as his favourite goal of all time. People had not seen anyone scoring goals in this style before.

Ten minutes later, Brazilian team player Zagallo broke the morale of the Swedish team by scoring the fourth goal. The Brazilian players could sense the approaching victory. Although, Sweden's Simonsson scored a goal eleven minutes before the end of the game, the Brazilians were certain of their victory.

The Brazilian supporters chanted, "Samba! Samba!"

The last goal was the most exciting one. Pelé hit the flying ball inside the net with his head.

There was no doubt any longer that Brazil had become world champions. Pelé was lying on the ground in front of the goalpost. Garrincha helped him restore normal blood circulation in his legs by moving them.

Meanwhile, the game was over. Naturally, Pelé became emotional. He was missing his family living in Bauru. Did they know that Brazil had won the World Championship?

Pelé wanted to talk to his parents immediately, but there was no phone facility at that time. He went on muttering, "I have to tell my father..."

Pelé was able to communicate with his parents the next day with the help of international radio. He said to his father, "Did you see me with the king of Sweden? Over. I shook hands with the king. Over."

After winning the match, all the players of the Brazilian team started crying. Pelé cried with his head on Gilmar's shoulder. Everyone cried together with joy and relief.

Meanwhile, physiotherapist Mário Américo grabbed the ball from the referee's hand and danced his way to the dressing room. The referee was upset with his action.

The players ran around the stadium waving a giant Swedish streamer. King Gustav VI of Sweden walked onto the field and congratulated the Brazilian players. Even though his country had lost the final, he lauded the Brazilian players for their excellent performance.

Swedish player, Sigge Parling, later said that he became a fan of Pelé's talent when Pelé scored his fifth goal.

A grand celebration was held at the hotel and a feast was organized. The players enjoyed the delicious food. A separate banquet was held at the Brazilian Embassy, but Pelé went straight to his room. He was thinking about how to tell his parents about his feelings.

After the defeats of 1950 and 1954, Brazil had finally managed to become the World Champion.

❑

Joy and Sorrow

With the victory of the 1958 World Cup, Pelé became world-famous overnight. Newspapers and magazines around the world began publishing his life story. Immediately after the victory, 'Paris Match' magazine published a cover story about Pelé, writing that a new 'King' had arrived in the world of football.

People liked the title 'King' and everyone started calling him 'King Pelé'. Pelé's friends believed that he was a 'King' in the true sense since the people had given him a place in their hearts.

The Brazilian team returned after the celebrations in Stockholm. All the players were exhausted. Everyone wanted to meet their families as soon as possible.

When the plane carrying the players first arrived at Recife airport in the eastern part of Brazil, the players understood the meaning of their achievement in the true sense. As soon as the door of the plane opened, the sound of cheering was heard. Despite heavy rain, a large number of people had turned up to welcome their favourite players.

When the team members reached Rio the next day, there was a festive atmosphere. Crowds had gathered on the streets. A grand procession was taken out with the players.

The then MP Assis Chateaubriand, who owned Brazil's famous magazine 'O Cruzeiro', radio stations and TV channels, took all the players to 'O Cruzeiro's' office, where the players' family members had already been invited.

Pelé's father Dondinho choked with emotion as he hugged his son. His mother, Celeste, congratulated him with tears in her eyes, "Congratulations Dico..."

Pelé's mother tearfully told him how she had missed him and how people in Bauru had celebrated after the World Cup victory and how Pelé's neighbours were now proud of Pelé's success.

With Brazil's victory in the World Cup, Pelé's mother knew that it was going to help her family. Dondinho, on the other hand, was proud of his son's success and forgot the pain of disappointment and failure in his career.

None of the players had expected to meet their family members in this manner and everyone felt happy at this noble effort of the MP. All the players were able to see their families in person after a long time. Many of the players had travelled out of the country for the first time in their life. Now all the players needed a break.

The whole country was celebrating. The team reached São Paulo the next day and was warmly received by the people. Everyone wanted to shower their love on the victorious players.

There were crowds everywhere. People raised slogans, cheered, waved hands and congratulated the team. The players took part in a grand procession. Everyone in the crowd wanted to shake hands with the players and congratulate them.

From the jubilation visible among the people, it was clear how earning the World Cup title was a moment of national pride for them. People were trying to express their gratitude to their players. All the team members were naturally overwhelmed with such love from the public.

The celebration went on for several days, with the team members attending a number of receptions, dinners, and banquets. Sometimes the players didn't even know who was hosting the reception, but that didn't matter.

Pelé was amazed to see the enthusiasm of his fellow countrymen. He felt good that he too had fought in that great victory campaign and had made his countrymen proud by winning the World Cup.

All the team members became popular stars overnight. Journalists would surround them and ask questions continuously, but the players were not used to answering questions in this manner. Pelé went to Santos to attend the reception with his teammates Zito and Pepe. With that, the official receptions came to an end and the players were asked to return to their homes.

Pelé had left Bauru only two years ago. At that time, he was a teenager dreaming of making a place for himself in the world of football. Today the same Pelé was returning to his hometown after winning the World Cup title.

Pelé's heart was beating hard. He imagined the warmth with which the people of his own town were going to welcome him. He had heard that the whole town was eagerly awaiting his arrival.

When Pelé got off the plane, he saw a crowd gathering around him. People waved, shouted, and welcomed Pelé. A group of photographers came running towards him. Among the crowd, Pelé also saw his parents and Uncle Jorg. He also saw his sister Maria Lucia and brother Zoca. All his childhood friends also were there to welcome him.

Pelé was taken on an open truck and a procession was taken out in the whole city. The city was well decorated. Familiar townspeople standing by the side of the road shook Pelé's hand and congratulated him. Nicola Avallone Jr., the mayor of Bauru, set up a stand in the main square to felicitate Pelé. The reception ceremony was organized at the same place. The mayor congratulated Pelé on behalf of the people of the city. People presented various gifts to Pelé.

Pelé's mother presented a medal to him. When the mother was asked to speak, she could not say anything. She kissed Pelé. Tears started flowing from her eyes.

When the flow of gifts ended, another big gift awaited Pelé. It was a three-wheeled vehicle 'Romiseta', which was very popular in those days. The vehicle was gifted to Pelé by the mayor.

The next morning Pelé woke up to find Romiseta outside, which the mayor's staff had left outside his house. The car now belonged to Pelé even though he was not old enough to obtain a driver's license.

Pelé touched the car like a small child. Then he called his father.

Pelé said, "This car is yours."

His father said, "What are you saying? It is not mine; it is yours."

Pelé said, "I am giving it to you as a gift. I want you to keep it."

His father was in a dilemma. He said, "But you have received it as a gift, you cannot give it to anyone else."

When Pelé told his father that he could not take the vehicle with him to Santos, his father said that someone else could deliver the vehicle to Santos.

Then Pelé said, "Don't worry, I'll sell it."

His father became angry and said, "You will sell it? Have you lost your mind? You can't sell something that you have received as a gift." Pelé said, "Then why don't you keep it?"

Then Pelé's mother reasoned with Pelé's father that Pelé could have an accident while driving in Santos. Eventually, Pelé's father agreed to his request, but he kept one condition, "Even though I am keeping this car with me, it is your property. Whenever you want, I will deliver it to Santos."

The victory in the World Cup changed the lives of his parents more than his. They were being invited to such parties and functions in Bauru, which they had not even imagined about attending earlier.

Pelé's parents also felt embarrassed attending such upper-class parties since their lives had changed very rapidly and they could not yet handle it.

However, there was no significant change in Pelé's life after he returned to Santos. He was still staying with his fellow players. Although people began to look at him with curiosity there was no significant change in his life. Pelé had joined Santos at the age of fifteen and nothing else distracted him except considering himself a football player.

Despite the World Cup victory, Pelé remained as involved and winning as ever. His life went on in the same way as before. He was still away from the glare of fame while playing with fellow players.

Due to the environment that he grew up in, he had to lead a disciplined life. Due to the nature of his contract, he was not paid much by the club.

Pelé always looked for ways to make some extra money. In the evening, the senior players would get together to play cards and bet money. Pelé did not take part in the game, but the senior players would order him, "Pelé, bring coffee!" Senior players would pay him to buy food and drink. In this way, Pelé would earn some extra money.

Upon his return from the World Cup tournament, Pelé had to compete in challenging football events. First, it was the São Paulo State Championship. Santos won the title in 1956, but it was won by the Palmeiras the very next year.

Brazil did not have a national league at the time since it was not considered practical to establish such a league considering the size of the country. Rio's bigger teams had their own league called 'Carioca' while Santos' league was called 'Paulistâo'.

The Paulistâo League was considered challenging, with teams such as Corinthians and São Paulo Rough Sea as its parts. Santos was on a winning streak that year. They won matches with scores of 10–0, 9–1, 7–1, and 8–1. Pelé scored a total of 58 goals in thirty-eight matches, which was a record for the 1958 championship, the year Santos won the title.

Del Bacio, a key Santos player, left Santos and moved to Europe to play. In this way, in his place, Pelé got the opportunity to play in the starting line-up.

Santos had only a handful of matches against Rio's powerful club Botafogo. Garrincha was a part of that club. Similarly, names like Vasco, Flamengo and Fluminense were parts of the famous clubs of Rio.

But from the early 1959, a small annual tournament was organized under the name of 'Rio-São Paulo', in which all the clubs got a chance to play against each other.

In 1959, Santos won this title for the first time. But that year, Santos failed to capture Paulistâo. However, from the following year, Santos won Paulistâo for three consecutive times and during this period Pelé scored the highest number of goals.

At that time, Santos was at the pinnacle of success. The forward line-up featured Pelé as well as skilful players such as Pepe, Pagão and Coutinho. Pepe had previously played alongside Pelé in the national team.

Pepe played with amazing pace and scored the highest number of goals after Pelé, but he could not get recognition at the international level. Pagão understood the finer points of the game very well. Similarly, Coutinho played the role of centre forward with efficiency.

Coutinho and Pelé had a great coordination on the field. Both exchanged quick-fire passes and confused the players of the opposing team.

In the Santos team, Dorval performed brilliantly like Garrincha while Zito performed brilliantly as a midfield player. Mauro played the role of central defence.

In 1962, Mauro was appointed the captain of the Brazil team. Gilmar was the goalkeeper, who had played in the World Cup. Santos' team was considered a charismatic team in those days. This team created a sensation by winning 85 percent of the matches played in those days.

A few months after the end of the World Cup, Santos against Corinthians match was scheduled. Before the start of such matches, there was a rule to keep the players isolated so that they would not lose focus. The day before the match, Pelé and his teammates were put up at Vila Belmiro.

One of the reasons for keeping the players isolated was also that they would stay away from the girls. But in spite of such arrangements, the players would find opportunities to socialize with the girls.

That evening, when the team members were feeling low, Pelé proposed to watch a girls' basketball match in the gym downstairs. Pelé went to the gym with four of his teammates.

There was a match going on between Santos' team Atlético Santista and São Paulo's team Corinthians. Some girls came forward to talk to the football players, but one girl remained seated on the bench.

Pelé was looking at the girl sitting on the bench. The girl also looked at Pelé. She got up and went to him.

"You are Pelé, aren't you?" she asked.

Pale said, "Yes." He felt happy that the girl recognized him.

"Do not beat the Corinthians badly in tomorrow's match."

Saying this the girl went back and sat on the bench. Pelé kept looking at her from the corners of his eyes. He found the brown-haired girl very attractive.

Pelé's teammates came to know that Pelé was attracted towards an unknown girl. They started pulling his leg. The girl was only fourteen years old. However, Pelé was only three years older than her. That girl had cast a spell on Pelé. Then she left for a changing room.

After Pelé returned to the camp with his teammates, he continued thinking about the girl.

The next day when the football match started, Pelé felt that the girl had definitely come to watch the match. Many times, he could not see the ball properly as he kept searching for her among the spectators.

But that girl had not come to watch the match. One day, Pelé met some girls from the basketball team on the way. Initially, Pelé thought that the girls were connected with the São Paulo team. But when he came to know that they were residents of Santos, he immediately asked for the name and address of the fourteen-year-old girl.

Her name was Rosemari. With the help of the address given by the girls, Pelé went to Rosemari's house in search of her.

After greeting her, Pelé asked, "If you are from Santos, then why were you sympathizing with the Corinthians?"

"Because I support Corinthians." She replied, "Anyway, I don't like football much."

Although, it didn't start off on an encouraging note, Pelé managed to get Rosemari to agree to a second meeting. However, Rosemari said that she was young and that it was not right for her to go out with a boy so young. So, it would be better if Pelé could go to her house on a Saturday to talk to her.

Pelé consented to Rosemari. Pelé wore a nice outfit and arrived at Rosemari's house. Rosemari's parents welcomed Pelé in a friendly manner. Pelé was the first young man to visit Rosemari at her home, and he was the first black visitor to their house.

Rosemari's mother Donna Idalina had baked some biscuits. Rosemari's father, Guilherme Cholbi worked at the Santos port and was a football fan. Pelé was happy to spend Saturday evening with the family. He felt at home in that family in a foreign city.

There were many such meetings between Pelé and Rosemari. This went on for months and years—the relationship had to go through a lot of hiccups. Rosemari's family did not want the media to know about this relationship. That's why whenever Pelé and Rosemari wanted to go to the cinema, an aunt would first take Rosemari to the cinema hall and when the lights went out inside the hall, Pelé could go and sit next to Rosemari.

Despite this, Pelé was extremely happy to be in Rosemari's company. Despite all the restrictions, Pelé fell deeply in love with Rosemari. He was thrilled to imagine the day when Rosemari would be a part of his life forever.

Pelé wanted to marry Rosemari, but he also had apprehensions. Rosemari was young and not interested in football. Pelé wondered whether Rosemari had really fallen in love with him or had merely agreed to befriend him due to his fame.

Faced with such questions, Pelé remembered his childhood days in Bauru when he had become friends with a Japanese girl named Neujinha. Neujinha's family did not care whether Pelé played football or not. Neujinha liked him as a teenager.

During the 1958 World Cup, Pelé had become friends with a girl named Ilina in Gothenburg. Ilina also did not give importance to the fact that Pelé was a member of the Brazilian national team in the slightest. There was a mutual youthful attraction between the two.

With such thoughts, Pelé analyzed his love affair with Rosemari and finally decided to marry her.

Meanwhile, Pelé also had to overcome the obstacle of the Brazilian army's rules. It is said that football is sometimes like war—especially the World Cup is no less than warfare. Pelé believed that he had fought valiantly in the war of football and led his country to victory in the World Cup held in Sweden.

Pelé celebrated his 18th birthday a few months after his return to Brazil from Sweden. Now the time had come for one year of compulsory military service. Pelé was not willing to spend a year in the army.

He told what was in his heart to the two directors of Santos. Both the directors were military men. Pelé reasoned, "I have fought for my country. I shouldn't have to join the army to fight a war again. I have done my part."

Both directors looked at Pelé and started laughing. One could be exempted from compulsory military service only on the ground of some disease. "Have you lost your mind?" they said. "How can we make an excuse that you have a problem with your lungs or have a broken leg? You have just won the World Cup. The whole country knows that you are perfectly fit. If you hadn't been so famous, it would have been easy to make an excuse, but your case can't be exempted."

Pelé was recruited into the 6G AC Army unit. This unit was in Santos only and Colonel Osman was in charge of this unit; he loved football, but he was also extremely disciplined.

While serving in the army, Pelé also took part in matches as a part of the Santos team and the Brazil national team. Pelé was not made to work much in the barracks he was kept. Being a skilled sportsman, he got some exemptions and facilities. At the same time, there were some military officers who expected Pelé to behave like a disciplined soldier. Pelé would forget that he was the world champion. Considering himself a common soldier, he would engage himself in activities like mowing grass, washing clothes, or polishing shoes.

Captain Aurino was in charge of the barracks where Pelé was kept. He believed in enforcing strict discipline. On the other hand, a military officer named Sergeant Kalous did not believe in giving any kind of concession to Pelé and assigned him additional responsibilities. Pelé later said, "These military officers were not bad people. They were just doing their duty."

The name of the in charge of the barracks football team was Lieutenant Falcao. He took his responsibility very seriously and treated the military players as if he was training a national or international team.

If a player played poorly during training, the lieutenant punished him by making him spend the night outside or by making him do more work. But the lieutenant treated everyone equally and in later days became friends with Pelé.

Apart from Pelé, the barracks football team featured some of the best professional players, including Lorico who played for the Portuguese de Desportos, and Celio and Lara who played for Jabaquara. Later Lara died of a heart attack during a match at Vila Balmeiro.

In the competition between the teams of different cantonments of Santos, Pelé's team often won. Teams from military cantonments in São Paulo also participated in one of the championships.

In November 1959, Pelé was selected as an Army XI player to play in the South American Military Championship. Army XI was playing against Argentina at Rio's General Severiano Stadium. In this final match, Pelé was sent off the field for the first time in his life.

Actually, an Argentine player was repeatedly pushing Pelé and trying to injure him. When Pelé could not tolerate it anymore, he also kicked him. A brawl broke out between the two and the referee sent both of them off the field. However, Army XI managed to win the final by 2–1.

The day after that match in Rio, Pelé had to play as a Santos player against Grêmio in Porto Alegre. Sometimes he had to play for the army team, and sometimes for Santos. As a result, he sometimes felt very tired.

Though, Pelé faced hardships while serving in the army due to rigorous physical exertion and a disciplined routine, he learned many useful new things.

The day he was sent off the field during the Rio match, Col. Usman told him, "You have to learn to control your anger. I know the Argentine player was attacking you, but the best way to defeat your opponent is with your skill."

As Pelé learnt the importance of discipline in military life, the feeling of patriotism also deepened in his mind.

As a result of winning the World Cup, Pelé's financial problems were also solved. Santos now agreed to pay Pelé more money through a new contract and thus Pelé bought a house for the family in Bauru.

Pelé's parents no longer had to worry about housing, nor did they need to pay the house rent anymore.

The World Cup victory also led to a rise in the income of the Santos club since now other clubs were eager to play matches with Santos. Brazil was internationally renowned for its football prowess, and the Santos club became a living example for the whole world.

The popularity of the players of Santos had increased and the club's management wanted to earn as much as possible due to this. Hence the team now started going on foreign tours regularly to play. At the beginning of the year, trips were made to American countries and in the middle of the year, trips were made to Europe.

The year 1959 was the starting year of such a busy tour. That year Pelé had to play for the Santos club as well as the army and the national team.

Pelé took part in 103 matches throughout the year and the five teams he represented were Santos, Brazil, All-Star São Paulo, Barracks Team, and Army Team.

On nine occasions Pelé had to play two matches within twenty-four hours, while on one occasion he played three matches within forty-eight hours. Santos' team played twenty-two matches in just six weeks during their first tour to Europe. So, the players did not get time to rest as they continuously played matches.

While playing in Europe, Santos won thirteen matches. Five matches ended in a draw and they lost only four matches.

Santos was defeated by Real Madrid, a team from Europe. At that time Real Madrid was considered the best team in Europe. This team had won the European Cup five times from 1956 to 1960.

When there was a match between Santos and Real Madrid, people started saying that only the winner of this match can get the status of the best club in the world. However, Pelé did not agree with this. "It was not fair to make such a claim. It was our 14th match on the tour and we were badly injured and tired," Pelé said.

Santos' second European tour was more of a relief to the players, as the number of matches was less than in the first. During this, Pelé got a chance to visit Egypt with his teammates.

When the plane stopped at Beirut airport on its way to Egypt, Santos' team was surrounded by a crowd. The crowd demanded that the Santos team must play a match with the Lebanese team. The mob threatened to kidnap Pelé if it failed to do so. Police intervened to disperse the crowd and the players reached Egypt safely. When the plane landed at Cairo airport, Pelé was surprised to find that the players were greeted with kisses on their lips. Pelé stood behind his teammate Djalma Santos. He noticed that despite being kissed, Djalma remained calm. Pelé also stood like a statue and remained calm even when people kissed him.

During this tour, when Pelé went to Paris to play, he met the model and actress Kiki there. Kiki took Pelé on a sightseeing tour of Paris. Both were together for many days. During this, press photographers took many pictures of both of them.

Pelé and Kiki had become friends. Pelé did not consider it as a romantic relationship. But his pictures with Kiki had also appeared in Brazilian magazines, and when he returned home, Rosemari also raised the topic of those pictures. With this experience, Pelé decided to be careful in future.

In May 1959, a football match between Brazil and England was held in Maracanã. Although it was a friendly match, the teams of both the countries took it very seriously. In fact, the Brazilian team was competing against such a strong team, which it had not been able to defeat in Sweden during the World Cup tournament.

A large number of spectators came to the stadium to watch the match. Most of those spectators had come to watch Garrincha play. Garrincha was not keeping well and coach Feola decided to field Julinho in place of Garrincha.

When Julinho's name was announced in place of Garrincha, spectators protested. But just ten minutes into the game, Julinho scored the first goal and silenced his critics. Later he also helped in scoring the second goal.

Now the audience started cheering for Julinho. They had forgotten Garrincha. At that time, the Brazilian team was so strong that it easily defeated any rival team.

During this period, Pelé had the opportunity to officiate as a referee in a football match. The match was played at Vila Belmiro between the referees of Santos and São Paulo.

Pelé said, "I had a sweet revenge over the referee and we celebrated that night."

The success that Pelé was achieving while playing for Santos and the Brazilian team was having a mixed effect on his younger brother Zoca. Zoca was also a good football player.

When Pelé moved to Santos, Zoca started playing with Bauru's Noroeste team. Zoca's reputation grew and the Santos management, showing interest in Zoca, spoke to Pelé about it. Pelé praised his brother's performance. Santos included Zoca in their team after testing his talent. Zoca went to Santos and started staying with Pelé and other players. He played for a few years as a reserve player and also appeared in matches as the main team member at times. But when Pelé played in the team, Zoca was not included.

Zoca had a promising future ahead of him. But one day he bid goodbye to football forever.

When Pelé asked him the reason for this decision, he said, "Whenever I play, reporters surround me and ask me questions only about my older brother Pelé. I want to leave sports to study and become a lawyer." Zoca later became a lawyer.

Pelé played continuously and also faced injuries regularly.

He was badly injured in February 1961. The Santos vs Nesxa match was held in Mexico City. Santos' players had travelled a long distance and, despite being tired, were braving the intense heat and fighting to win.

Santos was then trailing by 2–0. Then the Santos team scored a goal and the Santos players started playing enthusiastically. They started trying for at least a draw.

The ball was flying into the penalty box. Pelé and the goalkeeper jumped up at the same time. Pelé was hit in the face by the goalkeeper's forehead, while Argentine defender Elacho hit him on the shoulder.

Pelé instantly fainted. When the doctors of the team assisted him, he told them that there was darkness in front of his eyes. Despite this, he wanted to continue with the game. As soon as he stood up, he felt dizzy and fell down. Santos lost that match by 4–3.

Pelé did not sleep well that night due to headaches and facial and shoulder pain. He felt numbness on the left side of his face.

Pelé was admitted to a hospital in Mexico City the next morning. X-rays of his face and shoulder showed that there was no damage to the bones.

The Mexican media scoffed that Pelé was faking an injury as

he did not intend to play the next match and that Pelé was only interested in playing matches in Europe to earn more money. Pelé was deeply pained by such propaganda.

Pelé never resorted to excuses of any kind. He was ready to play in every adverse situation. He didn't see any difference between Santos or the national team, nor did he try to prioritize money.

Pelé was unable to play in Brazil's matches against Peru and Chile due to the injury and had to stay away from the game for three weeks.

After recovery when Pelé returned to the game, he played a decisive role in securing dramatic victories in matches against Guadalajara, America and Atlas.

By March, Pelé had fully recovered. Then in a match against Fluminense, Pelé scored a spectacular goal, which is considered the most spectacular goal of his career.

This match was played in Maracanã. Pelé controlled the ball with his feet from outside his side's penalty box and raced past all opponents towards the Fluminense goal, eventually getting past the goalkeeper and scoring a goal.

São Paulo's newspaper 'O Esporte' described this goal as the most beautiful goal scored at the Maracanã. This match was not broadcast on TV. That's why its memory remained imprinted only on the minds of the spectators present in the stadium.

To make that memorable goal immortal, a copper plaque was put at the entrance of the stadium by the newspaper which is called Goal with Copper Plaque. Whenever a new player scores a brilliant goal, Brazilian sports lovers praise him by calling it a 'copper-plaque goal'.

In June that year, Pelé was suffering from shoulder pain and was unable to leave on time for a tour of Europe with Santos' team.

When, after a medical examination, Pelé arrived to participate in the match in Basel, Switzerland, posters were put up in every corner of the city, on which it was written – 'Pelé has arrived and he is playing'.

Santos won the match by 8–2. Pelé scored five goals and Coutinho scored three goals. The Swiss spectators entered the ground as soon as the game was over. They wanted to tear the jerseys of the Santos players and take them as souvenirs.

The spectators were specifically targeting the jerseys of Pelé and Coutinho. Pelé and Coutinho ran into the dressing room. Then the crowd mistook two other black players as Pelé and Coutinho. The crowd surrounded both of them. Then when the crowd realized their mistake, they surrounded the Santos players and started shouting, "Where's Pelé! Where's Pelé!"

Later inside the dressing room, French journalist François Tabaud told Pelé, "I've never seen such rage before. People went berserk. You should see how the Brazilian game of football has been wholeheartedly accepted by the sports lovers of Europe."

In September 1961, Pelé scored twenty-three goals in six matches within three weeks. It was an impressive feat. Olympiacos were thrashed by 8–0 by Santos and Pelé scored five goals in the match.

Four days later, playing against São Paulo, Pelé scored four goals, then three days later, playing against Juventus, Pelé scored five goals. Santos won the match by 10–1. While playing against Botafogo, Pelé scored one goal.

On one occasion, Pelé was credited with a goal that had not actually been scored. The incident took place during a match against Guarani as part of the São Paulo Championship.

Pelé overshadowed the first two defenders, then fired past the third with a brilliant shot. The ball hit the crossbar, then fell to the ground and rolled off outside. Despite protests from Guarani players and fans, referee João Etzel Filho declared it a goal.

Etzel said, "Do you know one thing? It was such a fine display of sportsmanship that I could not help but declare it a goal. Whether the ball went in or not, Pelé scored and that is the final decision."

By this time, Pelé's popularity had reached its peak. Two books based on his life had been published, and a film titled 'I am Pelé' had been produced.

Pelé's popularity was not limited only to Brazil, he also had a huge number of fans in Europe.

A director of the Inter Milan club proposed to Pelé that he could earn 40 million cruzeiros if he agreed to play for his club. Pelé did not accept the offer. The Santos club was also not prepared to let go of Pelé at any cost.

When news of such deals spread across the country, the Brazilian Congress officially declared that 'Pelé was a national treasure who could not be exported at any cost'.

When the Santos team arrived in the city of Turin to compete in the Italia 61 championship, Fiat and Juventus club owner Avento Agnelli invited Pelé to dinner. Along with Pelé, the Santos' president Athiê Jorge Coury and some other dignitaries were also invited. Agnelli warmly welcomed the guests.

In the midst of the banquet itself, Agnelli asked Santos' president Coury, "Are you interested in making a deal to link Pelé with the Juventus club?" Coury was taken aback, while Pelé was also astounded.

Coury composed himself, "We can't sell Pelé. Buying him may prove more expensive than required."

Agnelli said, "How about if we start the bidding at one million dollars?"

Gradually Agnelli offered up to ten million dollars, but Coury turned down his offer. He knew that Pelé was invaluable and that Brazil could never make a deal regarding Pelé.

Pelé himself wanted to play for Brazil. He was still persuading Rosemari to marry him and had begun to apply for future financial security.

Pelé was now earning well in terms of Brazilian social status. Because of his popularity, Pelé began to earn extra money by associating his name with the promotion of products.

People started to believe that Pelé was earning a humongous amount of money. A man wrote to him from the city of Recife, "Mr. Pelé, I want you to buy me a car—it must be brand new and luxurious. I am a taxi driver and I want to sell my battered car."

Pelé was happy with his prosperity. While he felt a sense of satisfaction by making his parents happy, he was also worried due to the experience of his old teammate Vasco Calles. Vasco was crippled for life. Pelé wanted to secure his future.

Pelé consulted some well-wishers and decided to invest his hard-earned money in a business. He invested in a company called Sanitata. This company supplied construction materials.

A few days later, the 1962 World Cup was about to begin in Chile. While Brazil was the winner of the previous World Cup, it was also a strong contender for the 1962 title. The Brazilian team did a lot of preparation to retain the title.

During the tournament, the Brazilian team repeated the strategy adopted during the 1958 World Cup to win.

Feola had fallen ill. So, Aymoré Moreira was appointed the new coach of the Brazil team. However, there was no change in the list of team members and other collaborators.

Gilmar, Djalma Santos, Nilton Santos, Didi, Garrincha, Zito, Zagallo, Vava and Pelé, who had played in the previous World Cup retained their spots in the team. Mauro and Coutinho, who played with Pelé in Santos, were also on the team.

The head of the Brazilian team, Paulo Machado Carvalho, wanted the team to prepare in the same manner as they had before winning the cup in 1958, to retain the World Cup title.

Paulo took some interesting steps during preparation. He chose the same pilot of the Panair do Brasil plane to fly them to Santiago who had flown the Brazilian team to Sweden in 1958. The name of the pilot was Captain Bugner.

Now Captain Bugner was working for Varyag Aircraft Company. This company had acquired the Panair Company.

Paulo had put the Panair logo on one of the engines of the plane which was taking the Brazilian team to Santiago. Basically, Paulo wanted to repeat everything that was done in 1958.

Paulo believed in various superstitions and after the 1958 victory, he continued to wear a brown coat to win again.

There was only one thing that Paulo could not be sure of—whether the weather would be favourable during the flight was beyond his control.

When the plane left for Santiago, the weather turned bad en route. The plane started tossing. Most of the players became panicky, but Pelé remained calm and seated in his seat.

When Pelé was asked by his companions the reason for his sitting calmly, he said, "I believe in God. If the death has to come, no one can avoid it. So, what is the point in getting frightened?"

Pelé's companions thought that Pelé had lost his mind. They asked, "Don't you have a family?"

Pelé asked, "What do you guys expect me to do?" and remained seated in his seat quietly.

Gradually the weather got better and the danger was also averted. Everyone started joking about how the tossing caused the spoons to change plates while eating.

Pelé suffered a hamstring strain during the 1962 World Cup tournament due to playing excessive football. Despite his young age, Pelé began to feel muscle pain, and his discomfort worsened after playing a friendly match against Portugal.

Pelé told team doctor Hilton Gosling about his problem. He also informed physiotherapist Mário Américo about his problem about how he felt mild pain. But both did not consider the problem serious and Pelé continued to play.

Along with playing, Pelé also had to participate in rigorous physical exercises. No player was exempted from the exercise. Paulo Amaral was the team trainer, who often said, "Everyone has to exercise." If someone from the Technical Commission tried to interfere with his regime, he would say, "I know what I am doing. I cannot allow anyone to interfere in my work since I also do not like to interfere in anyone's work."

Amaral's relationship with the players had also turned sour. On one occasion, Nilton Santos refused to leap over the hurdle. When he was pressured, he angrily said, "I have not come to Chile to participate in the running competition."

In 1958, Pelé was unable to participate in the opening matches due to injury. This time also he was worried that in case he did not remain completely healthy, he would not be able to participate in the matches of the World Cup.

Brazil was placed in Group 3 along with Mexico, Czechoslovakia and Spain. Matches were held at the newly built beautiful Sausalito Stadium on the downtown Vina Del Mar beach.

Brazil was expected to easily qualify by defeating all the other teams in the group. But in the very first match on May 30, 1962, Brazil had to face a tough challenge from its rival team Mexico.

The Mexican team was playing with discipline and fearlessness. The Brazilian team had to change its strategy to deal with it. In the second half, the Brazilian team managed to score two goals. The first goal was scored by Zagalo through a header and the second goal was scored by Pelé.

Pelé scored this goal in a striking way. He dodged four opponent players and then went past the goalkeeper to score.

In the first match, Pelé did not have any unusual problems, but his back pain would not go away. When he came out of the ground, he was feeling very tired and was in pain due to muscle strain.

Pelé wanted to tell Dr. Gosling about his problem, but he was afraid that Gosling might not allow him to play because of his pain. Thinking thus, he did not tell anything to the doctor.

A few days later, on June 2, a match between Brazil and Czechoslovakia was played. Pelé wanted to spend the ninety minutes playing well. It was possible to reach the next round only by winning or drawing this game.

The defense line of the Czechoslovakian team was very strong. That's why the Brazilian players were asked to shoot from a medium distance.

Pelé started with enthusiasm and did not care about the back pain. But after twenty-five minutes his condition started deteriorating. Garrincha kicked the ball towards him. Pelé kept moving forward, controlling the ball with his feet. He shot and the ball hit the post and returned. Pelé wanted to shoot again, but he fell due to pain. Mário Américo ran towards Pelé. The score was still 0–0 and only 25 minutes had passed. If Pelé were to be carried off the field, the Brazilian team would have been in trouble as the rule of sending a substitute had not yet been introduced at that time.

Pelé clenched his teeth to overcome the pain and said that he wanted to continue playing. Even though he had trouble due to pain, he tried to hide his pain. He knew that due to this problem, he could have to be deprived of playing in other matches of the World Cup. On the other hand, playing in this match meant that he could face more challenges fighting against powerful Czech players.

Despite this, Pelé felt a kind of positive change. It was not that his pain was miraculously cured, but he felt that the players of the Czechoslovakian team understood his misery and helped him. Three players, in particular, stopped troubling him showing goodwill.

The Czech players could have taken advantage of Pelé's painful condition and badly injured him if they wanted, but instead of doing so, they adopted the strategy of giving respite to Pelé.

When the Czech players saw Pelé going forward with the ball, they did not try to stop him. They gave Pelé a free hand until Pelé was in a position to score.

Later, Pelé recalled the goodwill of the Czech players with gratitude and described their attitude as a unique example of 'fair play'. Even though the Czech players were also playing to win the World Cup title, they displayed their sportsmanship by showing sympathy for Pelé.

No goals were scored during the match and the result was a draw. When Pelé arrived at the training camp, he could not walk properly. Despite this, he hoped to recover within a week and return to the field.

When Dr. Gosling examined Pelé, his face turned serious. He said, "I don't think you will be able to play in the upcoming World Cup matches." Despite this, Pelé felt that he would recover and play in the tournament.

When Pelé was resting, Garrincha was with him consoling him. He said, "You cannot leave us in the middle like this. You have to get well and play alongside us."

Garrincha was very worried about Pelé and wanted to see him recover as soon as possible. He requested the doctors to send Pelé to his hometown of Pau Grande, where an exorcist woman could cure him. Garrincha had great faith in the paranormal power of that woman.

During that time, there were also rumours that Pelé and Garrincha were getting close to Elza Soares, a famous and beautiful Brazilian samba singer. Elza had come to Chile to perform and a director of the Brazilian team had introduced Elza to Pelé.

Elza and Garrincha became increasingly close, and people began to say that Garrincha had snatched Elza away from Pelé, although Pelé denied such reports as mere hearsay.

Brazil's next match was against Spain. It was the last match of the group, scheduled to take place only four days after the match against Czechoslovakia. The day before the match, Pelé requested Dr. Gosling, "Give me some painkillers. I really want to play the match." The doctor quickly replied, "No, I can't do that at all."

Pelé kept requesting, but Dr. Gosling was not ready to give him medicine. He said, "You should get treatment—that would be the right thing to do. I can't give you any painkillers—that way you can die. I know it's a World Cup match and you are a great player. But even then, I can't let you play."

In the training camp, other players from the team tried to console Pelé. They said that there was nothing to worry about and that everything would be fine.

The problem seemed serious to the doctor. He was being treated in the traditional way. For five days, Mário Américo made Pelé lie down and covered him with a hot towel. Pelé watched the Brazilian team win by 2–1 against Spain on TV lying down.

Amarildo was fielded in place of Pelé, who performed well.

Pelé felt that his condition had improved. When he tried to get up, he felt more helpless than before. He felt that it was because he was continuously lying down.

After three days, Pelé was able to walk and now the pain had also subsided. He thought that he would get an opportunity to play in the next match. Pelé started practicing with the ball inside the training camp. His hope was growing and his confidence was getting stronger.

But days passed and Pelé's treatment continued. During that time, the series of World Cup matches also continued. The quarter-finals took place between Brazil and England, with Brazil emerging victorious by 3–1. Garrincha played brilliantly in this match. The England team had skillful players like Moore, Greaves, and Charlton, but Garrincha had demolished the English defence line.

Three days later Brazil's semi-final against the host country Chile began. Pelé watched this match sitting in the stands. Pelé felt that due to the treatment, he had recovered to a great extent and if his team won the semi-final, he would definitely get a chance to play in the final.

In this match too, Garrincha displayed his skills remarkably. He did not give any chance to the rival players to dominate. He boldly led his team, scored goals and constantly tricked the rival players.

Garrincha scored two goals and dominated the match. Just then, some Chilean players pushed him and he got into a scuffle with them. The referee asked him to leave the field.

When Garrincha was leaving the field, some miscreant threw a bottle on his head and injured him. His wound had to be stitched. Despite this, the Brazilian team won. Vava also scored two goals and Brazil advanced to the final for the second time in a row.

Brazil was to face Czechoslovakia in the World Cup final. In the semi-finals, Czechoslovakia defeated Yugoslavia by 3–1. Pelé attended practice with his teammates. At that time, he did not feel any difficulty. He felt that he deserved to play in the final.

While running after the ball during practice, Pelé once again experienced excruciating pain. He had severe pain in his back. He was not even in a position to say anything properly. He realised that it was not possible for him to play in the final of the World Cup.

Pelé started crying out of helplessness. He had prepared so much to play in the World Cup, but due to physical inability, he was not able to play. He felt that it was his greatest misfortune to miss out on the second biggest match of his life when the second biggest match of his life had come up after a series of achievements for the club, army, and national team.

Pelé could not calm down. He requested the team management to send him home.

The team management wanted Pelé to be present during the final and contribute to raising the morale of his teammates.

Doctor Paulo said to Pelé, "If we keep discussing the possibility of your taking part in the final, our rival team will become more worried. They will have to change their strategy at the last moment as they would not know the line-up of all our players till the last moment."

Pelé could not argue the reasoning. He started boosting the morale of his fellow players. Even though he was not going to play in the final, he kept encouraging the team by giving useful suggestions. Brazil went on to win the World Cup final by 3–1 for the second time in a row.

The whole world began to know Pelé at the age of twenty-one itself. Despite getting so much fame, Pelé remained a humble and well-mannered person. He had not forgotten his roots. He always remembered the upbringing that his parents gave him. He soon recovered from the depression he suffered during the 1962 World Cup.

Pelé was always taken care of by his teammates in Chile. On his return to Brazil, the countrymen welcomed him warmly.

As soon as Pelé recovered, he had the chance to play for Santos in the final of the Libertadores Cup. He scored two goals. Santos went on to win the match by 3–0.

As soon as the match was over, Argentine sports-loving spectators rushed onto the field and tore off Pelé's clothes. It was a moment of triumph. Santos became the first Brazilian club to win this trophy.

❑

Target Man

Pelé returned to play for Santos in 1962 after returning to Brazil from Chile. His whereabouts had not changed either. He stayed with his teammates as before. During those days, football players could not even think of living in comfort like in today's time.

There may not have been any changes in the facilities, but Pelé's importance in the field had increased compared to earlier. He was no longer considered a newcomer. Rather he was considered a challenger. Pelé had become famous throughout the world due to his extraordinary performances for the Santos club and the Brazil national team.

In 1963, Pelé appeared in more than fifty matches for Santos abroad. The invitations that the Santos Club was receiving from different countries were not because other clubs had any sort of attachment to Santos or because other clubs wanted to learn about the rhythm, pace and creativity of Santos' players.

In fact, other clubs wanted to know the secret of Santos' strengths and wanted to find out the weaknesses of Santos' players. Not only that, the coaches of those clubs had planned strategies to injure Santos' players. They wanted to make use of force the rule in the field and wanted to resort to violence to some extent.

Several coaches instructed their players to use force against Santos' players. The art of football was going to suffer the most because of this erroneous thinking.

Many coaches had told their defenders to always surround Pelé on the field. This kind of strategy sometimes led to awkward situations.

On one occasion, when Pelé went off the field to tie his shoelaces, a defender followed him and stared at him with his hands on his waist.

Players from rival teams abroad as well as those in Brazil began to behave in a similar hostile manner. While there was always the danger of physical injury, there was also the possibility of mental harassment.

The players would mock each other or taunt and try to distract from the game. Players of the rival team especially liked to target a skillful player like Pelé.

In February 1963, a match was held at Maracanã between Santos and Vasco da Gama. Vasco was leading by2–0 with only a few minutes left in the match.

Just then, Vasco players Fontana and Brito started making fun of Pelé. Fontana said to Pelé, "Has the king lost his skills?" Brito said, "Where has the famous Santos player disappeared?"

At that moment, Pelé scored a goal. Despite this, Vasco's players did not stop jeering—since they were sure of their victory. But in the last minute, Pelé hit the second goal and made the score equal.

Pelé grabbed the ball from the inside of the net. He walked over to Fontana, handed him the ball, and said, "Take it to your mother. Tell her that the king has sent the gift."

Each country has its own distinct style of playing football, and Brazil also has a particular style. However, it has also undergone change and evolution over time.

The Brazilian style of football is characterized by ball control, short passes, and an attacking style of play that is both effective and spectacular.

Brazil-like qualities can also be seen in the performance of Argentina's players, but they have been placing more emphasis on the use of force. There has been a rivalry between Brazil and Argentina for years. That's why it is natural for the spectators to get emotional during the match between the two. In 1963, Santos reached the final of the Libertadores Cup for the second time in a row. The match was being played in Buenos Aires (Argentina) against the local team Boca Juniors.

The stadium was constructed in such a way that there was very little distance between the spectators and the players. The spectators were calling the Santos players 'Brazilian monkeys' in unison.

Some players of the Santos team were troubled to hear such racist remarks, but Pelé did not care about such things at all.

During the match, Argentine players were trying to cause injury to Pelé. He was pushed several times. Sometimes he was deliberately thrown down. He was kicked many times.

Then a player pulled Pelé's shirt from behind, due to which it was torn. In those days, there was no rule to show a red card for such behaviour. A team assistant brought a second shirt and Pelé lay down on the ground. He was surrounded by fellow players and he changed his shirt.

When Boca scored the first goal, there was a wave of joy in the whole stadium. But shortly after that, Coutinho equalized the score by kicking a pass from Pelé inside the net.

There was a war-like atmosphere in the stadium. Pelé scored the winning goal eight minutes before the end of the match. Santos once again won the South American Championship. Santos was now going to face AC Milan in the international club competition category.

The first match took place in Milan. Pelé scored two goals in the match, but Santos was defeated by 4–2 and Pelé also suffered an injury during the match.

The final match was held in Maracanã, in which Pelé and Zito could not play. But other players proved that they were not dependent only on Pelé and Zito. Santos won by 4–2.

Rio's spectators supported Santos whenever an international match was held in Maracanã. To show their gratitude to the fans of Rio, Santos decided to organize a friendly match against Fluminense.

Each Santos player wore the jersey of a different club in Rio. Pelé did not wear the jersey of any major club to show objectivity. Instead, he chose to wear the jersey of Olaria, a small club in Rio's northern suburbs.

Pelé used to feel happy while playing matches abroad. Foreign visitors used to welcome them warmly. Pelé and his teammates also had the opportunity to learn the nuances of football while playing abroad.

Pelé took a closer look at the European style of football. He found that England players traditionally preferred to pass the ball through long passes and dangerous crosses to the centre forward, who then scored a goal with a header or shot.

The style of play adopted by the Eastern European teams seemed to be very similar to that of the South American teams. Hungarian players played football in a particularly beautiful way.

Italian teams used to pay the most attention to defence. Most people used to call their style 'anti-play'. But with the help of this style, impressive results could be achieved during a counterattack.

Teams from Scandinavia, Belgium and Holland were adept at displaying collective mobility and unerring tactics.

Over time, European teams began to become unbeatable. Players started to become physically fitter, and under the defensive strategy, teams began to employ the skill of surrounding each and every player on the opposing team.

This siege prowess was also coupled with the use of on-field violence, which naturally made it difficult for Brazilian players to play football.

During one of the matches, when a player from the rival team continuously adopted an aggressive attitude towards Pelé, Pelé said to him, "Would you prefer to play football without attacking me or not? Let me tell you one thing, if I want, I can beat you too." Pelé's words had an effect and the player stopped following him.

Football players from Latin American countries do not like to resort to violence on the field. But with the passage of time, the prevalence of violence and use of force on the field has increased.

In this regard, Pelé says, "Can coaches be held responsible for promoting the use of force? Did they encourage players to commit violence? I can't say." I blame the referees, who misinterpreted the laws of the game and did not consider it necessary to punish those who committed violence.

In 1964, Santos appointed Professor Júlio Mazzei as the technical instructor. Mazzei was hired to look after all aspects of the physical preparation of the team's players.

Santos had hired Mazzei's services with a lot of difficulties. Prior to that, he had worked with the Palmeiras club in São Paulo for three years. He had helped the club win the Paulista title and he had also helped them win two matches against Santos.

Mazzei was educated in America and was a humble and intellectual person. As soon as Mazzei joined the Santos club, he made a remarkable contribution to improving the performance of the players.

Pelé and Mazzei gradually developed an intimate friendship. Some 45 years later, Pelé described Mazzei as his brother.

Mazzei changed the style of Santos' players. Mazzei was a seasoned coach. Along with that, he also knew how to solve the personal problems of the players.

Mazzei taught the Santos players how to behave in hotels, at airports, and in different cities.

In January 1965, the Santos team reached Santiago, the capital of Chile. Pelé had not been able to play in Chile in 1962 and he still regretted it. This time, he tried to console himself while playing in an exciting match.

Santos was competing against the national team of Czechoslovakia. This was the same team that had participated in the 1962 World Cup. The only difference was that Pelé was playing for Santos instead of the Brazilian national team.

A large number of spectators gathered in the stadium to watch the match. Pelé scored three goals as Santos emerged victorious by 6–4 in a thrilling contest. The next day the Chilean newspapers described the match as an 'unforgettable encounter'.

Pelé had become friends with Professor Mazzei. Mazzei explained to Pelé that he was no longer a teenager but an adult and that he was a senior member of Santos and the Brazil team. Along with sports, he also had a responsibility towards the family.

Encouraged by Mazzei's advice, Pelé came to the conclusion that the time had come to consummate his relationship with Rosemari. For seven years he had been friends with Rosemari. During this time, every time he mentioned marriage, Rosemari rejected his proposal, saying that it was too soon. Every time, she would say that she was too young for that.

One day, Pelé made Rosemari sit with him and mentioned marriage. Rosemari again said that they should wait a little. But this time Pelé didn't want to hear any excuses. He was supposed to go fishing with Rosemari on the weekend. He told Rosemari that he was going to propose marriage to her that day.

Pelé was sure that Rosemari's father would accept him as his son-in-law. He had personally witnessed over the years how patiently Pelé had loved his daughter. He also knew that Pelé's earnings were satisfactory and that he could keep Rosemari happy.

Pelé no longer stayed with his team members. He had his own large house near the beach now. Santos' contract required him to stay around the beach. All the members of Pelé's family had come to live in that house. The house was very large and Pelé's own old house at Bauru seemed too small in front of it.

Pelé considered himself fortunate to live under the same roof as his mother Dona Celeste, father Dondinho, uncle Jorge, grandmother Ambrosina, brother Zoca and sister Maria Lucia. Now he wanted to bring Rosemari to this house by making her his life partner.

On a weekend, Pelé went fishing with Rosemari's father, Guilherme, in a small boat. Pelé told him that he wanted to marry his daughter Rosemari.

There was no expression of joy or excitement on Rosemari's father's face when he heard Pelé speak. He shook his head and said, "We will see. I will discuss this with my wife upon return."

Pelé anxiously waited for the evening. After returning home in the evening, Rosemari's father told his wife Dona Idalina about Pelé's proposal and she was delighted. Idalina wondered why it took them so long to reach this conclusion. Eventually the marriage was fixed.

A few months later, in 1966, during Carnival week, Rosemari and Pelé were married. A simple wedding ceremony was held, which was attended by both the families and a few close friends.

The media spread various rumours about the wedding. One rumour was that the wedding was to take place in the presence of the Pope. (By the way, Pelé and Rosemari managed to get the Pope's blessing during their honeymoon). The second rumour was that a stadium had been booked considering the large number of guests.

Pelé was hurt by the media's attitude. Pelé was particularly upset when some journalists questioned the propriety of a black man marrying a white girl. Race had never been an obstacle in their love, but media persons were now determined to create a white-black divide.

After the wedding, Pelé and Rosemari left for Europe on their honeymoon. Holland Endler, a wealthy German businessman, paid for Pelé's honeymoon. Actually, Endler was a fan of Santos and Pelé. Later, he was also made an honorary member of the club.

Pelé and Rosemari were first hosted in Germany for initial few days. When Pelé and Rosemari went to any shop to buy something, the shopkeeper would refuse to accept any money. Pelé was overwhelmed by the love of the German people.

Pelé and Rosemari reached Austria after visiting France and Switzerland. In Austria, the mayor of Vienna hosted a second wedding ceremony in honour of Pelé and Rosemari. The two then travelled to Italy, where they were warmly received by Pope Paul VI in Vatican City. Rosemari was very happy to receive blessings from the Pope.

When Pelé returned to Santos with his wife after their honeymoon, he was very tired. In spite of that, he was very happy. There was no shortage of anything in his life now. Pelé moved into a luxurious apartment with Rosemari. His parents lived in a big house nearby. Pelé was performing brilliantly for club and country.

Around the same time, Pelé had to face the consequences of a bad investment decision. A few years ago, a businessman named Pepe Gordo had shown him dreams of a profitable venture, and trusting him, Pelé had made him his power of attorney.

A few months before the wedding, when Pepe Gordo approached Pelé and asked for money, Pelé could not understand why the man to whom he had entrusted all his savings, had come to him to ask for money.

When Pelé inquired about the problem, he learned that Gordo's investment in Sanitaria Sanrista, a company that produced building materials, had sunk.

Gordo told Pelé that he had lost all his investments and that he was in debt.

The money Pelé had earned through hard work, contracts and endorsements—Gordo squandered all his earnings.

Pelé had realized his mistake. He had blindly trusted Gordo and Gordo had taken advantage of this and driven him to the brink of bankruptcy.

Rosemari didn't like Gordo from the start and constantly warned Pelé. But Pelé didn't pay attention to Rosemari and now he had to suffer the consequences.

When Pelé got the full account of his investment with the help of experts, he came to know that even if he sold all his assets, it was not possible for him to repay the debt. He was advised to declare himself bankrupt. Pelé was not ready to accept this suggestion. He believed that by doing so he would be discredited by the people. Everyone considered him rich and people could misinterpret such a declaration.

Pelé decided to arrange for the money to pay off the loan. He wanted to repay the loan and regain prosperity anew by working hard. He explained his problem to the directors of the Santos club.

The directors agreed to give him the amount. But in return, Pelé had to sign an agreement with the club, where the terms were more beneficial to the club. Pelé had no other option. He had been associated with Santos for ten years and was the most famous player in the club. Despite this, he was not being given high remuneration.

After paying off the debts, Pelé immediately revoked the power of attorney given to Pepe Gordo. Learning from this mistake, he decided not to give power of attorney to anyone in the future.

In 1966, the World Cup was organized in England. Everyone was surmising that Brazil, which won the World Cup in 1958 and 1962, would become the world champion for the third time as well.

Brazil won the World Cup title in Sweden and Chile. The Brazilian players were eyeing the feat for the third time.

Sports fans in Brazil looked up to their players with anticipation. A wave of euphoria anticipating the victory ran across the country and no one was left untouched by such optimism. Similar optimism was visible among sports officials as well. They felt that their players would easily defeat everyone in the tournament and win the World Cup.

On the other hand, the Brazilian team did not prepare for victory like in 1958 or 1962. Brazil had to suffer the consequences of not paying attention to preparation.

After 1958, many new finest players emerged in Brazil. But illustrious players like Didi, Garrincha, Gilmar, Mauro and Nilton Santos could not easily be replaced by newcomers.

There was a lot of confusion in the process of selection as well. Too many players were selected for training. A total of forty players were selected for the practice session. Twenty of those players were not selected for the tour of England.

Amarildo and Jair da Costa who were members of the Brazil team in 1962 now played for clubs in Italy. The Brazilian team management had called both of them to play in the World Cup.

During the previous two World Cups, players playing for foreign clubs were not given a place in the team. Amarildo and Costa did not play in the World Cup tournament anyway as both were not physically fit to play.

Pelé later said, " I think we failed in the end because of building an army of too many players and displaying overconfidence."

After the players were selected, no fixed place was set for practice. The practice sessions were organized in different parts of the country.

Strict discipline is needed to keep any team united. It is necessary to keep all the players together and practice. The number of players that the Brazilian sports officials were trying to prepare for the World Cup equalled the number of players in four teams. Doing so was not proving practical.

When the players left Brazil, there was no cohesion among them as a team. Some players had already developed a sense of resentment about the attitude of the team management.

Vicente Feola had returned as the team manager, but he did not seem to be as effective as before. He did not show the same efficiency he had shown in the year 1958.

Dr. Paulo Machado and Dr. Carvalho had stepped down as heads of the Brazilian team and were replaced by Carlos Nascimento. He did not like to have any kind of conversation with Feola. Due to the lack of communication, a negative atmosphere was created.

Bruno Hamini was appointed as the new trainer of the team although the former trainer Paulo Amaral was retained as a member of the team management. Paulo probably did not trust Bruno's potential and was not able to utilize him properly.

Paulo never told Bruno how the team should be trained. Thus, the aspect of training was completely ignored.

There were a number of misunderstandings within the Brazilian contingent prior to their arrival in England. There was a lot of infighting, a lot of confusion, and uncertainty. Earlier in the tournament, when eleven players were selected for friendly matches, a trend of changing those players in the next matches continued.

The team management arbitrarily selected players without assigning any reason and fielded different players in different matches without coordination.

The situation took a turn for the worse when the team management dropped Carlos Alberto and Djalma Santos from the squad. Both the players were playing exceptionally well at that time. Even after reaching England, the list of players who were to play in the tournament was not finalised.

Even during the friendly matches that were played before the start of the tournament, no attempt was made to finalize the team. At the end of Jun, a friendly match was held between Brazil and Scotland at Hampden Park. The Brazilian team fielded Pelé, Gerson, Jairzinho and Servilio in the forward line.

Servilio was playing a technically superior game and had good coordination with Pelé and Gerson. All four players put up a strong fight although the match ended in a draw at 1–1. Servilio scored for Brazil.

But Servilio was removed from the team after the match without assigning any reason and was sent back to Brazil. The same treatment was meted out to goalkeeper Waldir as well.

The confidence of the Brazilian players began to waver. There was no team spirit and no one had faith in the technical commission anymore. The team management thought it easy to win the World Cup, but it did not pay attention to strengthening the team.

In this regard, Pelé later said, "So many mistakes were committed during the preparation for the World Cup that we should not have had a chance to win any of the matches in the tournament ... The way frequent changes were made, the practice was neglected, the change in weather and diet that was felt, the lack of preparation for the game, and the overconfidence of the officials—all these things led to our complete failure in England."

When Pelé reached England with his teammates, he found life there to be different from that in Brazil. He felt that people were driving the wrong way on the roads. He found this sight strange. It made him laugh.

During the tour of England, the players often joked among themselves to divert attention from the management's mistakes. Gerson and Jairzinho kept cracking jokes. Since Pelé did not know English very well, he would answer people's questions in monosyllables.

Brazil was to play all its group matches at Goodison Park in Liverpool. Once again, Dr. Gosling had chosen a good camp for his team, which was at Lyme, near Washington.

Despite all the facilities, the Brazilian players felt that their preparation was not satisfactory and that the team management had failed to find an effective solution.

The team management could not take proper decisions and tried to cover up its mistakes.

The contrast in cultures was also visible. The Brazilian team management enforced a strict code of conduct for its players as always. The sole aim of the players was to play in the World Cup. All the players had to stay in the hotel and obey the orders of the sports officials.

In the sixties in England, there was an emerging trend among young people to wear long hair and rebel against society. Before the start of the tournament, a journalist told Pelé that 'The Beatles' loved football and that they wanted to give a performance in honour of the Brazilian team.

Pelé had heard about 'The Beatles'. He told Feola and Carlos Nascimento about their proposal to perform. Pelé liked the idea and felt that music could energize the players.

Nascimento belonged to the older generation and was not impressed by the offer. He had not heard about 'The Beatles'. He said, "Are you talking about those boys with long hair? Look, you guys are here to play football and not for rock and roll. I will not allow this."

Ten years later, Pelé got a chance to meet John Lennon. At that time, he lived in New York and played football for Cosmos. He went to the Berlitz School near Central Park to learn English. Lennon was learning Japanese at the same school.

Pelé and Lennon were introduced and the two began to talk. Lennon asked him if he knew that in 1966 'The Beatles' wanted to perform for the Brazilian team and that the team management had turned down the offer. Pelé said, "I know very well. I had even asked for permission for it." Lennon told him that he loved football and admired Brazil.

On July 12, Brazil's first match took place against Bulgaria. Brazil fielded impressive players, which could be described as an extraordinary line-up.

Apart from Pelé, four members from the 1958 winning team were fielded: Gilmar as the goalkeeper, Djalma Santos in defence, and Bellini and Garrincha.

While Bellini was a reserve player in 1962, this time he had returned as captain.

Some people expressed surprise that Pelé was never appointed captain of the team. At that time, Pelé was only twenty-five years old. However, he had the experience of playing in two World Cups and had full plans as the captain of the national team.

But Pelé always turned down the offer of captaincy. He did not become captain of either Santos or Brazil national team or the Cosmos team.

The argument behind Pelé not becoming the captain was always that being a famous player on the field, other players and spectators respected him and the referee also gave importance to him. He did not need the authority of the captaincy separately. If another player was appointed the captain, then the dominance of two players could be maintained simultaneously on the field.

Brazil won the match against Bulgaria by 2–0. Pelé scored the first goal, while Garrincha scored the second. Both the players converted the free kicks into goals. Pelé's performance was highly praised by the English newspapers. Garrincha was not able to perform as well as before. A few days earlier, he was injured in a road accident and Dr. Gosling believed that he had not recovered fully.

This was the last match that Pelé played alongside Garrincha for the Brazilian national team. It was a coincidence that when in 1958, Pelé and Garrincha played for the Brazilian team for the first time, the opponent was also the Bulgarian team.

As soon as the team won, the Brazilian sports officials became overconfident. They felt that with the best players on the team, any opposing team could be easily defeated.

Sports officials ignored the fact that even though their team had excellent players, there was a lack of cohesion and coordination among the players. Without this quality, it was not possible to achieve success.

The Bulgarian players used excessive force on the field, and Pelé's foot began to ache during the match. While one of the reasons for this pain was lack of practice, members of the opposing team on the field also attacked his ankle many times or tried to push him down. When Pelé was being wounded, the referee made no effort to save him.

Team officials thought it best to rest Pelé to protect him from such attacks in the next match. The next match was going to be played against Hungary. Pelé considered the decision of the officials to rest him to be wrong.

Pelé believed that it was necessary to defeat Hungary and he was prepared to get injured in order to do so. Brazil could qualify in their group by defeating Hungary. Then even if Pelé did not play in the last match of the group against Portugal, it would not have made any difference.

The team management was convinced that Hungary could be defeated easily. A few more changes were made to the team. Tostão was fielded in place of Pelé.

In the first half, the score was 1–1. Tostão scored for Brazil. It seemed that the match was going to be a draw. But in the second half, the Hungarian players played brilliantly and took a lead by 3–1. Hungarian player Flórián Albert played brilliantly.

Hungarian player Farkas scored a goal. Then a goal was scored through a penalty kick. The Brazilian defence line appeared to be disintegrating. Brazil had expected to draw the match, but it had to face defeat.

Portugal and Hungary had four points each and Brazil had only two points. Now only the Almighty could help Brazil. Brazil had to win the match against Portugal by a huge margin. Only then Brazil could qualify in its group.

The Portugal team was coached by Brazilian veteran Otto Glória and it was a strong team. Most of the players of the Benfica club were included in this team and their morale remained high.

Before the match, there was a dilemma regarding the Brazilian team. No one knew which players were going to get an opportunity to play in the match. The list was revised till the last moment. The selectors had lost their balance.

Pelé was included in the line-up even though he was not fully fit. Gilmar was not in a position to play and was replaced by Manga as the goalkeeper. Manga was quite nervous because of the challenges.

Djalma Santos, Bellini and Garrincha were not going to play in this match. However, Orlando, who had played in the 1958 World Cup, was included in this match.

Manga's nervousness grew and he failed to prevent a goal just fourteen minutes into the game. He tried to stop a cross with a flurry of punches. The ball went to Simões, who headed the ball into the net.

Two minutes later the score was 2–0 as Eusébio also scored the second goal with a header.

In the second half, Rildo definitely scored a goal for Brazil, but Portugal did not feel any difficulty.

Eusevio also scored the second goal. Brazil lost the match by 3–0. With this, it was also out of the World Cup competition.

❑

Dream Tip

Pelé wanted to showcase his skills in the 1970 World Cup. In the three World Cups in which he had participated so far, he had not participated in all the matches. In 1970, Pelé was eager to participate in all the matches of the tournament.

He felt that he had to prove certain aspects of his skills, while the Brazilian team's officials had learned a lot from the bitter experience of 1966. They had decided that they won't make the same mistake again. It seemed to Pelé that the selectors had developed a clear vision of the challenges ahead.

Mexico was to host the 1970 World Cup. Pelé wanted to play in Mexico as the sports fans there loved him.

Actually, whenever there was a match between Santos and Guadalajara, the whole of Mexico would go on holiday. The posters on the streets made it clear whom the Mexicans actually supported. The posters said, "There will be no work today. We are on leave to see Pelé."

In Mexico, no other team was welcomed with so much enthusiasm as Brazil was. The other teams used to complain about the heat and the hooting by the spectators. But Pelé had no complaints against the Mexicans. To him, it was all about football. He was willing to go to any part of the earth to play it.

In 1969, Pelé and his teammates started training hard to prepare for the World Cup. But at the same time, the coach of the team made hostile comments against some players of the Brazil team, including Pelé.

The coach told reporters that Pelé would not be allowed to participate in the World Cup because of his blurred vision.

Pelé could not believe this. It was true that he had some difficulty seeing things up close, but his eyesight was not so bad that it would prevent him from playing.

Pelé's teammates called the coach's allegation fabricated. Carlos Alberto said, "Pelé is the player we all trust."

Pelé decided to answer the coach's claims in a lighter vein. He said that had his vision been strong, then by now he would have scored 2,000 goals instead of only 1,000.

The team management fired the coach and hired a man who had a positive opinion of Pelé. Zagallo had played with Pelé in the Brazilian team at the 1958 and 1962 World Cups. As a coach, Zagallo would listen carefully to the players on the team. Pelé liked this quality in Zagallo.

When the World Cup tournament began, Brazil won all six qualifying matches. Pelé was at his best. He scored six goals in six matches.

In fact, the members of the Brazilian team had been practicing for more than a year. All the players knew each other's strengths and weaknesses and showed excellent coordination during the matches.

The 1966 team was scattered, but this time there was unity in the team. Pelé said, "We understood each other very well. I think because of the mutual understanding, we were very comfortable."

The Brazilian team reached Mexico three weeks before the start of the World Cup tournament. The team went there early because the team management wanted the players to get used to the heat and humidity in the country.

Initially, the players encountered many difficulties while practicing. But with time, the team members became acclimatized to the adverse weather.

To make the Brazilian team the best, every aspect was paid special attention to, and efforts were made to leave no room for errors. Moreover, the jersey was also given a more attractive look than before.

The jersey was designed in such a way that it would not get wet due to sweat and the players would not have to bear the weight of a wet jersey. The jersey was designed according to the body size of each player so that none of them would have difficulty while playing on the field.

When so much attention was being paid to the clothes, some people were scoffing at such efforts. But Pelé was dead serious. "More than ninety million people are looking at us with the hope that we will return home with the trophy," he said.

The Brazilian team did not want to leave any gaps. While living together in Mexico for three weeks, a sense of camaraderie and harmony developed among the players. Pelé said, "We lived like a family and understood each other very well. In such a situation, there was no question of our failure."

On June 3, 1970, Brazil played a match against Czechoslovakia and began its campaign to win the World Cup for the third time. Despite the scorching heat, more than 50 thousand spectators were present in the stadium to watch the match.

When Czechoslovakia took the lead of 1–0 early in the game, Brazil's players were haunted by bad memories of the 1966 World Cup. Some journalists said that the Brazilian team was focused only on attack and remained indifferent to the defence.

The Czech coach had predicted that Pelé did not have the ability to play his best game anymore. When the Czechoslovakian team took the lead by scoring a goal, some people began to believe the coach's words.

But Pelé and his teammates did not lose their spirit. They had full faith in the power of their team and knew that it was not difficult for them to dominate the match. Just ten minutes after the first goal of the Czech team, Rivelino equalized the score for Brazil by converting a free kick into a goal.

Then came the moment that truly proved why the world calls Pelé the wizard of football.

The ball was under Pelé's control in the middle of the field. The Czech defenders moved to the back to block Pelé's attack. Pelé noticed that the Czech goalkeeper had left his position and had moved forward.

To everyone's astonishment, Pelé shot the ball. The ball went flying in the air and then came down and started rolling towards the net. The Czech goalkeeper ran quickly towards the net, but he was too late. It was his good luck that the ball had rolled some distance away from the net. The audience was awestruck. Pelé may have missed the goal, but his shot became memorable.

Pelé got another chance to score in the second half. He stopped the ball with the help of his chest and then sent the ball inside the net. Jairzinho scored two goals and thus Brazil won the match by 4–1.

Winning their first match was a great achievement, but the Brazilian team had no time to celebrate.

Brazil's next match was to be played against England, the defending champions of the previous World Cup and who were considered to be favourites for the title. The Brazilian team knew that its biggest challenge in the tournament was going to be the England team.

Around 70,000 spectators turned up at Guadalajara's Jalisco Stadium to watch the match between Brazil and England. The sun was scorching hot in the afternoon, but the Brazilian players were used to such heat.

Anyway, due to the cold weather in England, the players there face a lot of difficulties while playing in hot weather. On the other hand, in Brazil, players play in hot weather and get used to the heat.

Yet Pelé wanted to avoid overconfidence. "If they managed to score against us, I thought it would be impossible for Brazil to reach the quarter-finals," Pelé said.

Only ten minutes after the start of the game, Pelé was dominating one of the most famous matches of the World Cup. He kept running towards the goal. Then Jairzinho tossed the ball towards him from the right goal line. Pelé jumped up and headed the ball towards the net.

"I saw the ball dart into the net. I knew that it was a goal." Pelé said.

But just then the England team's goalkeeper Gordon Banks did something unexpected. He jumped and pushed the ball upwards using his fist and the ball went over the crossbar. Pelé was speechless and kept staring at Banks.

"It was an extraordinary save," Pelé said. Brazil goalkeeper Félix also praised Banks, saying, "It was the best save of the whole tournament".

Banks continued to prevent Brazil's attacks, but Pelé and his teammates remained patient and waited for the right opportunity. They kept the pressure on England. Brazil finally got their chance.

Pelé neatly passed the ball to Jairzinho and Jairzinho scored a goal. It was the only goal of the entire match. Brazil won the match by 1–0.

Brazil scored two goals against Romania in the first round of the finals. Brazil won but Pelé was not satisfied with his team's performance. He felt that all the team members had been overconfident and Brazil was simply lucky to win against a strong Romanian team.

Brazil's next match was against Peru. Didi, Pelé's teammate, was now the coach of the Peru team. Didi had given proper training to the Peruvian team and helped it make it to the World Cup tournament and Pelé praised Didi for this.

But the Peruvian team was very weak as compared to powerful Brazil. The Brazilian team wanted to play a match with a stronger opponent after playing a match against Romania. Since its performance was weak in the match against Romania, it wanted to return to the game with more vigour.

Peru was defeated by Brazil by 4–2. Pelé was satisfied with the performance of his teammates in this match. The team won the match with speed and rhythm. Both the teams displayed an attacking style of game and it was a fine display of football.

Brazil reached the semi-finals. The team members were eager to know which team they would face in the semi-finals. Eager as they were, the team members forgot to take shower and gathered in a room to listen to the commentary on the radio.

Pelé and his teammates heard that in the final moments of the match between Uruguay and the Soviet Union, Uruguay had scored a goal and won the match by 1–0. That means Brazil was going to face Uruguay in the semi-finals of the 1970 World Cup.

Analyzing the potential of the opposition, Pelé remembered the 1950 World Cup. That year, Brazil was considered a strong contender for the World Cup. It was the best team in the tournament and Brazil was also hosting the World Cup. But Uruguay defeated Brazil in Maracanã. It was a result that sent Brazilian sports fans into mourning. At that time, nine-year-old Pelé was also very sad. He wept for a long time.

In the 1970 World Cup, Pelé had a golden opportunity and could avenge the defeat of 1950. He could heal the wounds of his countrymen. His teammates felt the same.

Actually, the Brazilian players had become so emotional that they felt it was more important to defeat Uruguay than to win the World Cup.

"We didn't want to lose," Pelé said. "We knew that if we were defeated, we would not be able to face our countrymen in Brazil."

The date of the match arrived. Initially, Brazil failed to make an impact and Pelé's mind flashed back to the humiliating defeat of 1950.

He said, "We were making the same mistakes—bad passing, weak defence. We were not able to dominate our opponent." By then Uruguay was leading by 1–0. Pelé felt that this time over, they might face a humiliating defeat. But Brazil did not give up and kept up the fight. Pelé tried to score a goal, but the Uruguayan goalkeeper displayed amazing skill and made a brilliant save.

After some time, Pelé reached the penalty box with the ball. Before he could shoot, he was pushed down by a Uruguayan defender. Not only that, but the defender also crushed his ankle. Pelé looked at the referee for help. It was definitely a penalty. But the referee didn't pay any attention. Pelé got up and started playing.

Later, when Pelé was moving quickly, controlling the ball with his feet, he saw the same Uruguayan player who had pushed him running behind him. The defender was coming closer to him in an aggressive manner. Pelé understood that he would have to defend himself.

Before the Uruguayan player could attack Pelé, Pelé hit him in the head with his elbow. This time the referee blew the whistle. But the referee called for a penalty kick considering the Uruguayan player guilty.

Pelé did not like to attack the opponent players on the field and always tried to avoid such situations. But there were many moments when he had to defend himself. He has been proud of the fact that he has never been sent off the field for injuring a player.

The way Brazil had got a chance to dominate while playing against Peru, it was not getting a chance to take the lead in this match. But as soon as Uruguay scored the first goal it stopped playing aggressively and started shielding players by adopting a defensive strategy. Perhaps it was no longer interested in scoring more goals and felt that by scoring one goal it could win the match.

Uruguayan players were trying to stop the attacks of Brazilian players but it was not so easy to stop Brazil. The Brazilian players wanted to win this match at any cost. Shortly before the end of the first half, Brazil scored a goal to equalize the score.

Brazil desperately needed this goal. With this, the morale of its players was strengthened. All the team members heaved a sigh of relief as soon as the score was equal. The momentum of the Brazilian team had returned.

"We were controlling the game, we were playing great football with momentum," Pelé said. Jairzinho and Rivelino scored goals to put Brazil ahead by 3–1. With time, Brazil's victory became more and more assured.

In the final moments of the game, Pelé showed an example of his skill. One of his teammates kicked the ball into the Uruguayan penalty box. Pelé ran towards the ball. From the other side, the goalkeeper of Uruguay also ran to catch the ball. Before the two collided, Pelé moved to the left and was next to the goalkeeper.

The ball was on the right. Instead of catching the ball, the goalkeeper swooped down on Pelé. Now Pelé was left behind with the ball, but the two were on opposite sides. Pelé rushed towards the ball, lost his balance, but still shot the ball. The ball went flying and fell a short distance away from the goal.

A journalist from an English TV channel said, "Now we understand why people call this player the king, why Pelé is called the greatest football player in the world."

Pelé smiled. He didn't score a goal, but once again he showed his exceptional skill.

When the game ended, Brazil's vendetta was complete. Pelé said, "Our team was better than the Uruguayan team, as it was better in 1950, too. The only difference was that after twenty years, the better team had won, too."

Brazil could make history by winning another match. The same thing applied to its opponent as well. Italy had also won the

World Cup title twice. Whichever country won the final match would become the first country to win the World Cup three times.

This match was going to be exciting. The Italian team was famous for its strong defence. On the other hand, the Brazilian team believed in the mantra of attack. Sports lovers from all over the world were looking forward to this match. More than a billion people watched the match on television, and the World Cup was broadcast on colour TV for the first time. A million spectators turned up at the Azteca Stadium in Mexico City to watch the thrilling contest.

The Italian players focused on the defence. But they also had to find opportunities to score to beat Brazil. It was Italy's misfortune that Pelé and his teammates were at the peak of the game with their enthusiasm and energy.

Pelé later said, "It was one of my best matches that I had played wearing the Brazilian jersey." Only twenty minutes after the start of the match, Pelé was able to break through the strong Italian defence. Rivelino passed the ball to Pelé who was present in the penalty box, and Pelé headed the ball into the net to score the first goal. But thirty-seven minutes later, Italy also scored a goal to equalize the score.

Forty-four minutes later, Pelé again shot the ball into the net. But before that, the referee had blown his whistle and declared half-time. Pelé couldn't believe his hard luck.

Sports lovers speculated that due to the equal score, either team could have an upper hand in the second half. Some people thought that the Brazilian team would perform poorly out of despondency.

But the Brazilian players maintained their composure. They continued to attack, displaying discipline and concentration. Eventually, Gerson kicked the ball inside the net through a long shot. Brazil took a 2–1 lead. Five minutes later, Jairzinho also scored a goal. Now the lead was 3–1.

Pelé and his teammates realized that they were in control of the game. The Italian team's defence was faltering and its players were in no position to counter-attack. The Brazilian players were convinced that they had won the World Cup.

This was Pelé's last World Cup final match. He played a great game and before the end of the game showed why he was called the greatest football player in the world. He straightaway passed the ball to Carlos Alberto, who shot the ball into the net to make it a lead of 4–1. Shortly after, the referee blew the whistle to announce the end of the match.

Brazil had won the World Cup for the third time. The joy of the Brazilian fans in the stadium knew no bounds.

Spectators started running inside the stadium. They wanted to tear the jerseys of all the players and take them with them as mementos.

Pelé said, "I took my jersey off to make sure my head was protected." The crowd lifted Pelé on their shoulders and ran around the entire stadium. Eventually, the Brazilian players somehow made it to the locker room to celebrate.

Pelé went to take a shower and during that time he kept thinking about the achievement of the World Cup. He remembered all the hard work and struggle he had put in for so many days to achieve this memorable feat. He remembered his family and how the family had always stood by him through thick and thin.

Then Pelé returned to his teammates. All the team members reached the ground to accept the trophy. It was natural for every member of the team to get emotional at that time.

Pelé said, "As soon as Alberto held the trophy high above his head, his tears started flowing. Those were tears of joy. I had never seen such an emotional moment before." At the same time, Pelé's World Cup career also came to an end.

Pelé had completed a great journey. He fulfilled his resolution by playing in every match of the 1970 World Cup tournament. He said, "I realized that I had got everything I wanted in life."

He reflected on his performances in the matches he had played so far and did not regret anything. There was definitely a twinge though. It would have been great if he could have scored using his bicycle kick.

The team members had returned home to attend receptions and banquets. Some people were unable to accept Pelé's decision. They couldn't understand why Pelé, who had played excellent football, had announced that he would not participate in the World Cup again.

But Pelé had made a decision and he knew that his decision was absolutely right. Pelé said, "I have helped Brazil win the World Cup three times. I have played my part. I believe that now new players should get a chance to showcase their skills."

Pelé was very happy as he celebrated the victory with his countrymen. But he was exhausted. He missed his wife, who was pregnant at that time. She was waiting for Pelé to return home. Pelé went home.

On August 17, 1970, Rosemari gave birth to a son, Edinho. Pelé was very happy about becoming a father and started making plans for the future. He wondered how he would spend his life after giving up football.

Pelé didn't want to be just a football player. He wanted to learn and educate himself and he wanted to be a role model for his children.

Pelé felt that he had not paid enough attention to his studies as a child. He had left his studies at the junior high school level at the age of fourteen and started working to support the family financially.

After consulting with his wife, Rosemari, Pelé decided to resume his studies. He had to go through many tests before getting admission to college. When Pelé was not playing football, he was studying diligently. It was not easy to concentrate on studying after such a long gap. But slowly making efforts, he kept moving forward on the path of learning.

Pelé was quite nervous before one of the tests. His old friend Professor Júlio Mazzei was accompanying him. Mazzei said, "Don't worry Pelé! Keep calm. You have worked hard and studied diligently, there is nothing lacking in your preparation. If you don't think about failure, then you will not have any kind of anxiety."

Pelé pulled himself together and passed the test. Eventually, he got admission to Santos University. He studied physical education during the day and played football at night.

When he received his graduate degree, he felt proud of himself. He studied diligently and made his dream of educating himself come true. In 1971 Pelé decided to retire from the national team. He now wanted to spend more time with his family. He remembered his father's statement, "You should retire when you are at the peak of your career because the world would like to remember you as a player at the peak."

One thing was certain—Pelé had reached the peak at that point. He had won the World Cup three times and scored more than a thousand goals.

Brazil organized two matches to bid farewell to their popular star. The first match was held in São Paulo against Austria. Pelé only played in the first half, but scored his last goal as a member of the national team. It was his 77th goal in the yellow jersey of Brazil, a record for the team.

The second and final match was held at Maracanã. There were over 180,000 spectators in the stadium. The match between Brazil and Yugoslavia was drawn with a score of 2–2. But people did not care about anyone's defeat or victory. People had come 'to see the King play for the last time'.

In this match too, Pelé took part only in the first half. He was disappointed with his performance. He said, "It was not the best performance of my career. Actually, I became very emotional. I understood that I was not going to play in the Brazilian jersey again."

When the match was over, the spectators chanted in unison, "Don't leave! Don't leave! Don't leave!" Pelé started running on the field crying. He said, "I will never forget the amount of love shown by the audience."

Although, Pelé's career as a national team player was over now, he remained a Santos club player. In 1972, the Santos team travelled around the world. Pelé played his 1,000th match for Santos in Suriname.

Throughout the year, Pelé played matches in different countries and attracted the attention of football fans. He felt exhausted due to constant traveling and playing and was desperate to return to his family.

Pelé could not separate himself from Santos. He continued to play for Santos till 1974. Then he decided to leave Santos. Santos' management tried hard to dissuade Pelé, but he had made the final decision.

Pelé's last match for Santos was against Ponte Preta, a team from São Paulo. Nothing extraordinary happened for twenty minutes. Then suddenly Pelé caught the ball with both hands.

All the players came to a standstill. The crowd went silent. Everyone looked at Pelé. He ran to the centre circle and went down on his knees. He spread his arms and looked at the spectators in each part of the stadium. Tears welled up in his eyes as he saluted the spectators.

The audience stood up to show their respect. People started hailing Pelé in unison. Finally, Pelé stood up. He had become very emotional. It was difficult for him to stay in the field for another moment. He ran towards the locker room. There was one thought in his mind at that moment and it was that at the age of thirty-three he had already played the last match of his life.

After retiring from football, he realized that the game had become a part of his life and he missed it when he was away from it. But he was travelling continuously.

By the end of 1974, Pelé began to feel that he could now live a free life. He could earn the benefit from the investment that he had made in different businesses. He could easily earn a living and in such a situation, there was no question of having any kind of obligations.

Along with achieving economic independence, Pelé wanted to provide accurate guidance for football in Brazil. At the same time, he wanted to teach football skills to children around the world. Now he couldn't imagine returning to a team and playing football again—nor did he see such circumstances.

But this time, the commercial aspect forced Pelé to change his mind. Pelé had invested in the Fiolex company and that company was facing a crisis. When Pelé analyzed the situation with the help of experts, he learnt that he had suffered a huge financial loss because of the company. In fact, Pelé had signed a note for the company after thinking about it first. Using that note, the company had taken a loan from the bank which it could not repay. The bank held Pelé responsible for this. In this way, Pelé was surrounded by a financial crisis.

Pelé not only had to return the bank's amount but also had to pay the fine. Pelé entered into an agreement with the bank to repay the loan and sought help from FIFA President João Havelange. Pelé had helped João during his presidential election. Pelle wanted to save the Fiolex company from bankruptcy again. Pelé could not think of a solution since it required a lot of money.

Pelé certainly knew that if he started playing football again, his economic crisis would be easily resolved. After retiring from the game, he was receiving offers from different clubs.

Juventus and Real Madrid had even made an offer of $15 million to Pelé. Similarly, AC Milan and Mexico's America Club had also been offering him to play with them.

Pelé was unable to decide on lucrative offers from various European clubs. As a matter of fact, he was not interested in going to Europe. By joining a club in Europe, he might have had to play for a year and face constant pressure. He was not ready to start anew the same life that he had spent with the Santos club.

When Professor Mazzei saw Pelé in a state of confusion, he suggested that Pelé should consider the proposal of the Cosmos Club of New York. Cosmos had first proposed to Pelé in 1971 and was still ready to welcome Pelé.

Shortly after Pelé played his last match for Santos, Clive Hatoy from Cosmos phoned him, urging him to join the club. Pelé knew that Cosmos could be ready to accept his conditions.

Pelé discussed with Júlio Mazzei whether moving to America might prove favourable for him.

Pelé was also concerned that his decision to move to America might have a backlash in Brazil. He had announced his retirement from the national team as well as football, too. Pelé was also criticized for not playing in the 1974 World Cup. His critics argued that Pelé was physically fit and could have contributed to winning the World Cup by being part of the Brazilian team. But Pelé did not agree with this argument.

Now Pelé was about to announce his return to the world of football, and this could lead to reactions among his countrymen. Pelé also faced other difficulties in deciding to move to America. His English was not good. Apart from that, his family could also be affected by this decision. It could have an adverse effect, especially on his daughter Kelly Cristina.

Professor Mazzei resolved Pelé's doubts by assuring him that the purpose of his return to the world of football was to popularize football in America, the most powerful country in the world. Pelé and his children would also have the opportunity to learn English. In any case, knowledge of English would prove useful to him in the future. The amount offered by the Cosmos club was going to solve all the financial problems of Pelé.

❑

Back from Retirement

At the age of thirty-four, Pelé was thrilled to be back on the field again. Pelé said, "When I retired, something inside me died. Playing football again was like therapy for me."

But it took several months for the terms of the contract to be finalized. Eventually, the deal between Pelé and Cosmos was signed. Pelé, the wizard of football, was now ready to face a new challenge—he wanted to increase the popularity of football in America.

Pelé had previously toured the United States several times as a member of Santos' team. Rosemari had also visited New York City and liked it. Pelé said, "Rosemari was attracted by the many features of New York. The city had facilities for shopping, theatre, and museums. What's more, the phones in that city never went out of order. Such facilities could not even be imagined in South America."

But there was one problem—Pelé could not converse in English properly. But Professor Mazzei could speak English fluently. So, Pelé arranged for Mazzei and his wife also to join him in New York so that he would not face any language difficulties there.

On June 11, 1975, the Cosmos introduced Pelé as their newest player. A press conference was held at Manhattan's famous 21 Club. There was a crowd of reporters and photographers. Everyone was thrilled to hear the news that the popular Brazilian player was going to showcase his skills in America. Pelé tried to answer all the questions satisfactorily. Professor Mazzei played the role of interpreter.

While the media was excitedly promoting the news of Pelé's return from retirement, Pelé was trying to assess the abilities of his new team.

Pelé watched the match between Cosmos and Vancouver, which Cosmos lost by 1–0. He accompanied Cosmos' team to Philadelphia, where Cosmos again suffered a loss.

Pelé understood very well that it was not going to be an easy task to turn the Cosmos team into a winning team. Pelé said, "It was clear that a lot of work was needed to improve the team's performance."

Finally, the moment that everyone had been waiting for had arrived. The match he played as a Cosmos player for the first time attracted the attention of football fans around the world.

In that first match, the Cosmos defeated the team from Dallas. Pelé also hoped that the team's performance would gradually improve. But Pelé and the Cosmos continued to struggle in other matches during 1975. The Cosmos won ten matches and lost twelve throughout the year.

The performance of the players was disappointing. The quality of the game in America was much lower than the quality of the game that Pelé had seen in Brazil. Most of the Cosmos players depended on Pelé and were Pelé's fans. The Cosmos player Werner Roth said, "It had become our habit to watch Pelé mesmerized as he played, which distracted us from the game."

Even in such a hopeless situation, Pelé resolved to polish the players of his team like diamonds.

When the regular season of the competition was over, the Cosmos team left for Europe and the Caribbean region to participate in some exhibition matches. The team had its qualities and shortcomings. But the team members continued to improve their performance while playing together.

When Pelé joined the Cosmos team, the other players of the team were stunned. They had never imagined that they would ever have the opportunity to play on the field with Pelé, the wizard of football. That was the reason why, like fans, they would pass the ball to Pelé and watch his skill in awe.

All the players in the team expected Pelé alone to do the job of winning on the field. To change this atmosphere, Pelé advised all players to attack and try to score goals. He started encouraging the team members on the field.

Pelé openly praised other teammates when they performed well. He wanted all players to consider themselves as important as they considered him.

Over time, the confidence of the Cosmos players grew stronger. They no longer expected Pelé alone to score goals, but attacked with the ball themselves. Slowly the Cosmos team started playing football with pace and rhythm.

Rosemari also felt good in New York. Rosemari chose a swanky apartment in Manhattan, and Pelé's family moved into a new home.

Both the children had learned English. Pelé's son Edinho was a sports lover like his father, but he preferred to play baseball and basketball rather than football. When Edinho was sixteen, he even won a prize at school.

Pelé was invited on stage by the school's principal during the prize distribution ceremony. The principal requested Pelé to give the award to Edinho personally. Pelé agreed to present the award thinking that Edinho had won the football competition. "I first learned on stage that my son had won the Best Baseball Player award. I was surprised to hear that."

Pelé was beginning to like the new city—and the people of the new city were beginning to like Pelé. He was meeting celebrities, including singers Frank Sinatra and Mick Jagger.

Pelé wanted to raise the popularity of football among the younger generation of America. On the other hand, for the people of America, Pelé was synonymous with football. Hence, he continuously gave interviews to newspapers and magazines.

Pelé would often attend baseball and basketball matches to create awareness about football. He felt that his presence would automatically attract people to football.

Pelé was pleased to see that his efforts were beginning to pay off. Now a large number of spectators started coming to the stadium to watch football matches. Along with this, Pelé's fame was also growing. Wherever he went, people welcomed him warmly.

In 1976, Pelé was ready to play a full season as a Cosmos player. He expected an improvement in the performance of the team and this time, his expectation of victory was also high. But Pelé was also worried about some of the changes. Ken Furphy, a Britisher, was appointed the new coach of the team. Pelé did not find Furphy suitable as a coach. Furphy preferred to play football in a defensive style. Pelé did not like this style and felt that Furphy was making a mistake. Pelé said, "I believed that Furphy was incapable of motivating the players. He only wanted to teach the defensive style."

The acrimony intensified when Furphy ordered Pelé to be moved from the forward position to midfield. A forward's job is to score goals, and it was for this role that Cosmos had brought Pelé to New York. Furphy wanted to remove Pelé from that important role.

Out of the first five matches, the Cosmos won three matches. It was not a disappointing start, but Pelé was expecting a more outstanding performance from his team.

However, the confidence among the players had returned. Now instead of fumbling, they started playing football in a decisive manner.

The team's strength grew even more when the Cosmos club signed Italian striker Giorgio Chinaglia. Pelé appreciated the decision. He knew that the team desperately needed an attacking approach and Chinaglia was like a goal-scoring machine.

Pelé said, "When Chinaglia was included in the team, I began to see hope for future victories."

Chinaglia impressed the spectators in his very first match. He scored two goals. Pelé also scored two goals. The Cosmos went on to win the match by 6–0.

Now the situation was rapidly turning positive. However, the Cosmos managed to win only half of the next eight matches.

The feeling of frustration was increasing among players. Pelé knew that progress was not up to his expectation. There was a dire need for change in the team.

Gordon Bradley was the coach of the team when Pelé arrived to play for the Cosmos in 1975. But by 1976, he had assumed another role for the team. As the season wore on, the team's performance continued to falter.

Eventually, Furphy was fired and Bradley was reappointed as the coach. Pelé and his teammates were reassured by this change. They had won seven out of the last eight matches.

Playing against Miami, the Cosmos won by 8–2. Chinaglia scored five goals, while Pelé scored two. The Cosmos team, with its delayed vigour, took second place in the Northern Division competition. There was a marked improvement in the performance of Cosmos.

Pelé knew that the true potential of the Cosmos players could be tested through the playoffs. Some of the Cosmos players could handle pressure well because of their experience playing in Europe and South America. But Pelé wanted to see how the other players would handle pressure situations.

In the first round, all players handled the pressure with courage. Pelé scored a goal and the Cosmos defeated the Washington Diplomats by 2–0. Following the win, the Cosmos were set to play against the division winners, the Tampa Bay Rowdies.

There was a lot of curiosity among the football lovers of America about this match. Tampa Bay was the best team in the North American Soccer League (NASL). The match was being held in Tampa Bay, where the Rowdies had not lost a single match all season.

But football wizard Pelé wanted to introduce American sports fans to the skill and magic of football. He knew that with the help of his skill, he could affect the outcome of ten types of matches.

More than 40 thousand spectators gathered to watch the match. Tampa Bay was leading by 1–0 and then Pelé equalled the score with a goal.

The other Cosmos players struggled during the match. The Rowdies players were very strong and they played football with confidence. The Rowdies scored two more goals and won the match by 3–1. Pelé left the field. He was sad, but he had not lost hope.

Pelé said, "It was such a disappointing end to a season of hard work. But along with it came great progress—the performance of the Cosmos improved and the fascination for football rose among the people of America."

Now the future of football in America was starting to look bright. The number of spectators during the matches kept increasing and the matches were televised regularly.

New generation across the country was beginning to join soccer leagues. Pelé's dream of popularizing football in America began to come true. Now the people of America really started liking football.

Pelé had been playing football for more than twenty years. His name was in the record books. When Pelé was only thirty-six years old, he was considered a veteran in the world of football.

That is why Pelé told Cosmos that the 1977 season would be the last season of his career.

Pelé had proven his talent and skill to the world. But there was still one goal that he wanted to accomplish. He wanted to win a league championship to bring joy to his New York fans. He also had an opportunity to accomplish this goal.

At the start of the season, the dream of winning the championship seemed impossible. There was a lack of concentration among the Cosmos players. There were players from different countries on the team and they all played football according to the style prevalent in their respective countries.

Coaches had a hard time finding a style that all players would be willing to adopt. Pelé was beginning to get frustrated. Meanwhile, Fort was on its way to winning the Lauderdale Division.

Pelé started trying to organize things. The Cosmos management made several significant changes at Pelé's behest. In May the Cosmos signed World Cup champion West Germany team captain, Franz Beckenbauer.

In June, the Cosmos hired a new coach, but that did not seem to make any difference. Last season was slipping out of Pelé's hands. Then miraculously, there was a flow of energy among the Cosmos teammates.

Actually, Pelé was personally involved in motivating the players of the team through his performance. He was playing better than he did in previous years, and seeing his impressive performance, enthusiasm spread among the other players of the Cosmos.

The Cosmos management also signed Pelé's old teammate Carlos Alberto. In this way, the team's defense became stronger than before. Pelé was pleased with this decision. He knew that because of Alberto, Cosmos' way could become smoother. Now everything seemed favourable to him for a victory.

Once again, the spectators were excited about the match. A large number of spectators gathered at the Giants Stadium in

New Jersey. The Cosmos stunned the spectators by winning eight matches.

Now the Cosmos was inching closer to winning the title. Pelé could feel the victory approaching.

In the first round, the Cosmos played against rival team Tampa Bay. Cosmos had suffered a defeat at the hands of the same team last year. But this time, the rival team was not able to cope with Pelé and his team full of fervour. The Cosmos defeated Tampa Bay by 3–0 in front of over 55,000 spectators.

The next match was scheduled with the division's winner, Fort Lauderdale. The Cosmos defeated Fort Lauderdale by 8–3 in front of 78,000 spectators. Then in the semi-finals, Cosmos defeated Talkster.

This was followed by the NASL Outdoor Championship match held on August 27 in Portland, Oregon. The Cosmos defeated the Seattle Sounders by 2–1. Chinaglia scored the winning goal nine minutes before the end of the game.

Now Pelé was about to leave Cosmos. He had played 111 matches for Cosmos and scored 65 goals. To make the farewell memorable, Pelé visited Japan, Venezuela, Trinidad, China and India with the Cosmos team and showcased his skills in those countries.

Upon his return to America, a farewell match was scheduled to take place between Cosmos and Santos. In this match, Pelé was going to play on behalf of different teams in both halves. It was a very emotional occasion for him. Both his favourite teams were about to see him off after competing against each other.

On October 1, 1977, three weeks before Pelé's 37th birthday, 75,000 spectators gathered at the Giants Stadium to watch that memorable match. Pelé was about to bid farewell to football.

Millions of viewers watched this match on TV. Pelé scored for the Cosmos in the first half, but could not score for his favourite team Santos in the second half. Thus, the Cosmos won by 2–1.

The moment of farewell had arrived. Just as he had cried while bidding farewell to the Brazilian team in 1971 and Santos in 1974, his eyes were once again filled with tears amidst the cheers of the spectators.

Just then it started raining and Pelé did not try to wipe away the tears. This was the second club in his life which he was leaving. Pelé stood on the field and poured his heart out to the spectators. In the end, he said, "Love! Love! Love!"

Later, the Brazilian singer Caetano Veloso composed a song inspired by this moment of farewell. The song had one line—'Pelé said love, love, love.' Although many songs were composed about Pelé, Pelé especially loved this song.

Carlos Alberto tried to console Pelé, but Pelé was sad. The players lifted him on their shoulders and went around the entire ground.

A party was organized after the match. Apart from Pelé's parents, other relatives and friends also attended the event. Along with many famous football players from all over the world, boxer Muhammad Ali also attended the event. At the end of the match, Muhammad Ali wrapped Pelé in his arms and said, "Today the two greatest men have met."

Later, Pelé was asked why he took retirement. He mentioned his father's advice that one should always retire after reaching the top. Pelé was the champion as a member of Santos, the army team, and the Brazilian national team, and each time he left when he was at the top. He had also decided to leave only after making Cosmos the winning team.

Till then, Pelé had played 1,367 matches and scored 1,283 goals. It was an extraordinary achievement as a player.

❑

The World Citizen

On September 27, 1977, the United Nations honoured Pelé with the title of 'Citizen of the World'.

Pelé was deeply moved by the honour since at the time he was looking for a way to do something outside of football. He had decided to retire. Although he had signed several business and sponsorship deals, there was a certain restlessness in him.

He spoke about his feeling at the time, "When I received the honour of World Citizen, it helped me concentrate on my thoughts. It is true that every citizen of this earth can consider himself a world citizen. But when I was honoured with this title, I felt that I should create my own identity among the masses. I have carved a place in the hearts of people around the world through football. It is my good fortune that God has given me the talent to play, loving parents, and the opportunity to play with the best players in the world who have helped me in improving my skills. I had been playing football continuously for twenty years and the time had come to use the fame gained through this game in a positive way."

Pelé was appointed a member of the 'FIFA Fair Play Board'. Pelé was friends with the then FIFA President João Havelange and Pelé had helped him in his election to the presidency. Pelé supported the practice of yellow and red cards in the 1970 World Cup. While he wanted to promote high standards in the field of refereeing, he also wanted to strictly punish players who injured opponents on the field instead of playing.

Pelé had great respect for players who played with dignity on the field. He especially liked England player Gary Lineker. Lineker did not face a single yellow card during his entire career. Pelé considered Lineker a role model for professional players. In addition to serving as a member of the Fair Play Board, Pelé also began playing the role of FIFA's ambassador. He travelled around the world promoting football on behalf of FIFA.

Pelé was appointed as 'Goodwill Ambassador' by UNICEF. UNICEF was founded in 1946 to help children suffering from hunger and disease around the world. Pelé started participating on behalf of this organization in programmes organized to raise funds. Many years later, in November 2001, Pelé participated in a joint FIFA and UNICEF event, where it was announced that the 2002 World Cup would be dedicated to children around the world.

In 1978, Pelé's wife Rosemari gave birth to their third child, Jennifer. Pelé was in Argentina at the time. He had received the contract for commentary in the World Cup that year. Pelé wanted to gain experience in this area. He felt that in the future it could become a means of income.

Pelé regretted that he couldn't be with his wife during the birth of their daughter. Rosemari was very upset about this. Rosemari told him that she was not going to tolerate his absence. On one hand, Pelé was busy with his role as a UNICEF ambassador, on the other hand, a lot of his time was spent fulfilling advertising contracts.

Rosemari's argument was that Pelé had become busier than before since giving up playing, and she was now seeking a divorce.

It was true that Pelé remained away from home for eight months of the year due to his contracts for a variety of events. He was well aware that it was not an easy task for Rosemari to bring up three children on her own.

Pelé found Rosemari's arguments reasonable and they parted ways while deciding to remain friends. He also decided to continue to play an active role in their children's upbringing.

Thus, after twelve years of married life, Pelé and Rosemari officially announced their separation. Even after that, Pelé continued to support his ex-wife and take care of their children.

A few years later, Rosemari decided to publish a book about her relationship with Pelé. Pelé was hurt by the news. All three of Pelé's children and Pelé himself opposed Rosemari's decision.

Rosemari also went on to mention in her book that while she was having an affair with Pelé before their marriage, Pelé also had a relationship with another woman, which led to the birth of a daughter named Sandra Regina Machado.

Sandra was born in 1964, while Pelé and Rosemari were married in 1966. Sandra's mother Anisia Machado was domestic help.

About this episode, Pelé said, "When Anisia first brought Sandra to my house to meet me, I was already married and I refused to accept her claim to be the father of the girl since I had physical relations with Anisia only once. Beyond that, we had no relations. I was taken aback and naturally was not prepared to accept her since there was no proof that she was my daughter. Later, after many misunderstandings and arguments, it was proved that she was indeed my daughter and a court allowed her to add my title 'Nascimento' to her name." But the controversy did not end there. Sandra also decided to write a book titled 'The Daughter the King Didn't Want'. Naturally, Pelé felt hurt.

In fact, there was no communication between Pelé and Sandra till 1991. Initially, Pelé's sister Maria Lucia met Sandra and found that Sandra was more interested in money.

After marriage, Pelé's affair also continued with a journalist named Lenita Kurtz for a few days, who was a resident of Rio

Grande do Sul. This was the incident of 1968. As a result of this love affair, a daughter named Flávia Christina Kurtz was born.

Flávia was not interested in money. She liked Pelé as a father. Flávia's mother did not file a case against Pelé. When Pelé's mother first met Flávia, she immediately recognized her as her granddaughter. The decision to separate from Rosemari was proving painful for Pelé. He regretted that he was not able to spend time with the children. Then he decided to stay in New York. He signed a ten-year contract with Warner for advertising assignments.

Living a lonely life, Pelé started going to parties and befriended new people.

During that time, he met the beautiful model Maria da Graça Meneghel, who was of German origin and was famous as Xuxa. She had first met Pelé when she was sixteen years old. Pelé did a photoshoot with Xuxa in Rio for 'Manchette' magazine. At that time, apart from Xuxa, two other models also participated in the photoshoot.

Pelé took Xuxa to a concert with her father's permission, and the two grew closer.

Pelé helped Xuxa build her career. He introduced her to some filmmakers who used to make potboiler films. Xuxa got a chance to play the role of the leading lady in one such film and then the famous magazine 'Playboy' signed a contract with Xuxa for a photoshoot.

In late 1982, Xuxa became the cover girl of 'Playboy', and because of her fame, Xuxa was signed to present her own show on Manchet TV.

Xuxa's show on TV was related to children. Pelé felt that Xuxa's colorful past was not conducive to children's shows. Pelé talked to Xuxa, her parents, and 'Playboy's' management about it, and made an offer to help Xuxa—Pelé would give an exclusive interview to the magazine and in return, the magazine would give the negatives of all of Xuxa's nude and semi-nude photoshoots. Later he handed over all the negatives to Xuxa's parents.

Xuxa was relieved by Pelé's initiative as she no longer had the fear of the pictures going public. Xuxa achieved considerable success through TV shows. Later, she also appeared in the role of a singer and actress. Pelé and Xuxa lived together for six years.

Pelé's friendships with many beautiful women became well-known. He was close to Deise Nunes de Souza and Flávia Cavalcanti, who won the title of Miss Brazil.

After separating from Pelé, Xuxa moved in with motor racing champion Ayrton Senna. Ayrton died on May 1, 1994. Pelé was deeply saddened to hear this news. Just a day before, Pelé had married Assiria Seixas Lemos. It was his second marriage.

In fact, during this period, Pelé befriended many models and beautiful women, but he decided not to marry again. He changed his mind when he became friends with the Brazilian-born singer Assiria Seixas Lemos. Assiria was married at that time.

After several years, Assiria divorced her husband and decided to settle down with Pelé. Pelé and Assiria got married in 1994. Two years later Assiria gave birth to twins Joshua and Celeste. Pelé named his daughter Celeste after his mother.

After that, Pelé returned to Brazil to be with his family. He served as Minister of Sports from 1995 to 1998. He separated from Assiria in 2008.

When Pelé retired from football, the number of his goals had reached 1283. Despite this, in his later years, he continued to play football and score goals intermittently for various causes such as charity. However, those goals are not counted among his official goals. But according to one estimate, he scored an additional 100 goals. Counting those, the number of his goals is said to be 1375.

One of the main reasons behind Pelé's decision to come back after his first retirement and join the New York Cosmos club was that he wanted to increase the popularity of football in America.

His name evoked magic and his personality attracted people like a magnet. Wherever he went in America, crowds of people would gather to see him. People wanted to meet him, talk to him, and especially watch him play.

In retrospect, Pelé's three years with the New York Cosmos were highly successful. He had elevated his team to the status of a champion and it was a historic event at that time when he played in front of 78,000 spectators at the New York Stadium.

In the long run, Pelé's statement that America was a sleeping giant in the field of football and that the popularity of football among sports lovers was going to rise in the coming times proved to be true. But it took a long time for Pelé's prediction to come true.

With Pelé's help, the foundation of the North American Soccer League was laid, but for many years this organization did not make any significant contribution. Millions of dollars were spent and efforts were made by passionate individuals who had vision and dedication. A campaign was launched to connect the youth with football and in this way, football was popularized among the masses.

The North American Soccer League was founded in 1968 through Pelé's efforts, which was defunct by 1985. It took many years to revive this institution. In their childhood, American football players had drawn inspiration from the performances of Pelé and other popular players of the era.

In 1994, America hosted the Football World Cup. At the time, it was believed that FIFA had taken a risk by allowing the US to be the host since no professional leagues existed in the US at the time.

Despite this, the World Cup held in America was a tremendous success, and in 1996, Major League Soccer was born in place of the North American Soccer League. After this, the achievements of American players started coming to the fore in international competitions and football became a popular sport. Pelé personally saw football gain popularity in America.

Playing as a centre-forward, Pelé always wore the number 10 jersey on the field. Pelé was probably asked about the secret of his greatness many times over many decades. There was also a question related to this as to how a centre-forward player could become great.

Pelé, who avoided this question, made a list of the great players whom he considered the best a few years ago.

Pelé defined the center-forward as "someone who is a goal scorer, initiator, marksman, and team player. He is also ruthless and selfish and greedy because there is pressure of achieving his goal on him. The fear of failure controls him. If he fails, he can be ridiculed, people can hate him. On the other hand, if he is successful, fame and pride await him. This is the reason why we are a different species."

Even after his retirement from football, no other player has been able to challenge Pelé's greatness. However, he has been compared with Maradona from time to time. Pelé praised Maradona and said, "Maradona is the best player in the world in the eyes of many people. In fact, very few players can perform the way he charismatically performed in the tournament in 1986. He motivated his teammates to win and won all the matches on his own strength."

❑

Family

When Edinho, Pelé's eldest son, was born, Pelé thought that his son would grow up to be a footballer like his father and grandfather. As a child, Edinho showed interest in sports. He grew up in New York. There, he became interested in America's popular sports, baseball and basketball.

Occasionally, Pelé also gave football training to his son. Edinho performed better as an outfield player. Then he began to show interest in the role of goalkeeper. When Pelé's family returned for a one-year holiday, Santos tested Edinho and signed him as a goalkeeper.

Edinho remained associated with Santos for five years. He played with enthusiasm. He was 5 feet 10 inches tall and it was not easy for him to be the goalkeeper. But he would stop the ball with agility.

When Santos ended up as runners-up in the Brazilian National League in 1995, Edinho was the team's goalkeeper. Pelé always wondered how his son became a goalkeeper. Earlier he would always make fun of goalkeepers who wore a number one jersey. Now, he felt as if God was playing a joke on him.

Pelé's friends told him that Edinho had decided to be a goalkeeper so that people would not compare him with Pelé on the field. Pelé understood this pain very well. His brother Zoca had to face a similar situation and then Zoca bid farewell to football.

While playing in 1996, Edinho injured his knee and had to stay out of the field for a year and a half. Edinho jokingly said to his father, "You played football for twenty-five years and were never injured seriously. I only played football for four years and got injured badly."

Pelé also jokingly replied, "Son, I've been rough with goalkeepers all my life. I have been hurting them. Today you are suffering the consequences of my actions."

Edinho's wound healed, but he was not as agile as before. In 1999, he retired from football.

This aggrieved Pelé. He had confidence in his son's abilities and believed that his son could play as a member of the national team. But Edinho's career was cut short due to a knee injury.

After giving up football, Edinho started taking part in motocross races. He even produced a Motocross show on a Brazilian TV channel for some time, but destiny had other plans for him.

In 1970, when Edinho was born, Pelé had written a few lines at that time. These lines would trouble him later. He wrote, "The youth always think that they are superior to the elders. Sometimes they start walking on such a path, which they should not walk on. I want to warn young people that excess of anything is harmful—which often starts with smoking and drinking. I believe that young people can preserve their individuality even by belonging to a group, they can stand firm without being influenced or following anybody. Bad youths mislead good youths into the dark world of drugs."

When Pelé wrote these lines thirty-six years ago, he could not have imagined that one day his son would go down the wrong path. Edinho too was misled due to the company of bad friends.

In the seventies, Pelé was away from his home most of the time and due to this reason, his first marriage broke up. Pelé later said that his family was facing a lot of struggles while living in New York. Edinho lived with his mother and two sisters.

Edinho got married and had two daughters. In October 1992, Edinho became involved in an illegal car race case. A motorcyclist was killed during this car race.

As he was not directly responsible for the accident, the court sentenced Edinho to one and a half years of an open prison. The case was re-opened in 2005, in which the court acquitted Edinho, declaring him innocent. The court said that Edinho may have been in the car, but the car was being driven by someone else.

Edinho learned a lot from this experience. But during that time, he became friends with some wrong kind of people. Those selfish friends only wanted to take advantage of Edinho or wanted to get their work done with his help as he was Pelé's son.

One such friend of Edinho was named Naldinho. Naldinho was actually the son of Pitko, a former Santos player. Pelé had played alongside Pitko. Later, he also invited Pitko to play with the Cosmos.

Naldinho was facing trial for selling drugs and lending money on interest. One day he was arrested. Edinho was also arrested on June 6, 2005 as he was friends with Naldinho.

Excise officials raided Edinho's home in Santos, where he was living with his wife Jessica and two daughters. The officers did not find anything incriminating, yet they arrested Edinho.

The arrest was made by the authorities on the basis of telephonic conversations. However, crime could not be proved on that basis.

When Pelé was informed of his son's arrest, he thought that it was a nightmare. But it was not so. When he saw his family upset, he was convinced that the news was true. Pelé had never imagined such news. He had campaigned against the drug trade throughout his life. But now his son was arrested under the allegations of drug dealing.

Edinho was kept under high security at the Presidente Bernardes prison in São Paulo province. For two months, he was kept imprisoned there like a criminal who has committed a heinous crime.

Pelé's mental anguish went on increasing. He felt shame, fear, doubt, sadness and anger. He wanted to change the situation. He wanted to talk to Edinho. He wanted to give advice to his son about life. In this hour of crisis, Pelé was missing his father, Dondinho, who had passed away in 1996. Pelé felt that if his father was alive, he would have comforted him, held his hand and shown him the right path.

Pelé's mother Dona Celeste was a woman of strong will. But due to her advanced age, it was necessary to take care of her. She was saddened by the arrest of her grandson. Along with her grandson, she was also worried about her son.

As a father, Pelé grew restless. He would cry. He could not sleep properly. He kept asking himself, why all of that was happening to him? He never drank alcohol or smoked cigarettes; he had always fought against drugs. Then why was he facing such a situation? He felt that there was no point in being famous. Fame can sometimes prove to be a curse.

The government was taking precautions so that as the son of Pelé, Edinho would not get any kind of concessions. The government did not want to hear that Edinho was treated leniently because he was Pelé's son.

Pelé was in despair. He could only see darkness all around. In this hour of crisis, his wife Assiria, family and friends supported him.

Pelé hired lawyers and tried to save his son. He did not know anything about the court and its proceedings. He had only played football all his life. He answered questions from reporters and faced the camera.

Edinho was transferred to Tremble Penitentiary. This place was close to home. Pelé continued his travels. While he had to fulfill his contracts and promote the anti-drugs messages, he was also able to keep himself busy by traveling.

He felt that by keeping busy, the hour of crisis would pass quickly. He realized that he could not change the harsh reality of life. He resolved not to let himself become weak.

The new facility where Edinho was kept had better facilities and arrangements to keep the prisoners engaged in various activities. Edinho's daughters could now visit him without the need to go through heavy security checks. Pelé felt a little relieved.

Pelé kept blaming himself first for what had happened. Finally, he came to the conclusion that he did not have to repent or have a sense of guilt. He consoled himself that he was devoted to football throughout his life. He could not give enough time to his children since his profession required him to play continuously. But he made sure that his children did not face any kind of deprivation.

Pelé did not want to form any opinion about his son. He wanted to see his son released. He wanted his son to start a normal life afresh. But it was not in his control.

Now, the judicial system had to decide on the basis of the evidence that Edinho was completely innocent and that Edinho had no ties to his opportunistic friends who were connected with drugs.

In this regard, Pelé said, "I was miserable because of this sad episode. But I have faith that God will continue to guide me, as He has always been guiding me. If God has given me pain, then He probably knows that I will be able to get rid of this pain. God knows I have a sportsman's heart, which will bear the pain."

Pelé was overjoyed when Edinho was released in December 2005. The government announced that Edinho would remain free during the trial.

When Edinho returned home to celebrate Christmas, Pelé became emotional as a father. He spent a lot of time talking with Edinho. Edinho had become weaker and more sensitive than before.

Edinho would cry often. He knew that his problems were far from over. The trial was not over yet. He wanted to prove his innocence. He wanted to convince the judiciary that he had nothing to do with the drug trade.

Before the new year, Pelé accompanied Edinho to a clinic where drug addicts were treated. It was located about an hour from São Paulo.

In fact, Pelé went there at the request of his son. Edinho wanted to analyze his life and give up his addiction to marijuana forever. He wanted to get treated and lead a healthy life. But in Feb 2006, Edinho was arrested again, along with six other people.

Edinho's troubles brought members of the Pelé family closer together. Pelé has several homes where members of his family would gather. He has an apartment, an office and a villa in New York. The villa is in East Hampton, where both of his older daughters live.

His daughter Kelly Cristina is married to Arthur DeLuca. Cristina works in theatre and knows several languages. Pelé became a maternal grandfather for the first time with the birth of Cristina's son, Malcolm Edson.

His other daughter Jennifer also lives there. She works as an auditor in a digital film company. Having lived in New York continuously for a decade and then intermittently, Pelé feels that New York is his second home.

When it gets cold in New York, Pelé prefers to live in Brazil, where the weather is always warm. Pelé has an apartment and an office in São Paulo. Pelé lived there with Assiria and the children.

In the last phase of life, Pelé started spending more time with his family. He believes, "I think the family should be given the highest priority. As we grow older, our outlook on life also changes. Today I need my family members the most."

Pelé considers his family to be an important factor in his achievements. He believes that he was blessed with ideal parents who guided him in the right direction and taught him the lessons of life.

Pelé has been playing football with his young son Joshua. In doing so, he recalls his childhood, when his father Dondinho used to teach him the skills of football.

Pelé believes that all members of his family are blessed with longevity and that he too will have the opportunity to live a long life.

Pelé's grandmother Ambrosina died in 1976 at the age of 97. His father died in 1998 at the age of 86.

There is still a glimmer of hope in Pelé's eyes. He says, "It seems that in the coming days, I will lose my momentum. There are many benefits of getting fame. I have also got fame, but fame means nothing without family."

❑

Death

On December 29, 2022, the great footballer, Pelé died at the age of eighty-two. He died at Albert Einstein Hospital in São Paulo, Brazil. He was regarded as one of the greatest football players to exist and he was famously called "The King".

Almost a year before his death, Pelé was admitted to Albert Einstein Hospital to undergo surgery to remove a tumour on the right side of his colon in September 2021. In the last few years, Pelé had fragile health and he had trouble walking. Hence, he has been using a wheelchair and walking stick for ease.

In one of the routine cardiovascular and health checkups, the tumour was found on the right side of his colon. He was already battling with kidney problems when his cancer was diagnosed. After the surgery, he underwent chemotherapy to get rid of cancer completely. Later, he underwent a second surgery for the tumour in his colon in December 2021.

In late November 2022, Pelé was again admitted to Albert Einstein Hospital for "general swelling", along with respiratory infection and concerns with his chemotherapy as he has stopped responding to his treatment.

In December 2022, Albert Einstein Hospital announced that Pelé's cancer had worsened and that he had been placed under "elevated care" due to kidney and cardiac dysfunctions.

At that time, Pelé's daughter Kelly wrote in one of her posts on her Instagram that "We decided with the doctors that, for various reasons, it would be better for us to stay here with all the care that this new family at Einstein gives us. We, as always, thank you for all the love you show us here in Brazil as well as around the world! Your love for him and your stories and prayers are a huge comfort because we know we are not alone." She continued, "We wish everyone who celebrates Christmas is filled with family full of children and tons of love and health."

Pelé was honoured by his fans at the 2022 FIFA World Cup before he passed away. He died a week later after getting admitted to the hospital. His daughter Kelly confirmed his death through an Instagram post saying, "Everything that we are, is thanks to you. We love you infinitely. Rest in peace."

Pelé's death was mourned by the whole world. Many famous football players commented on his death. Neymar wrote in his Instagram post, "Pelé changed everything. He transformed football into art and entertainment. Football and Brazil elevated their standing thanks to the King! He is gone, but his magic will endure. Pelé is eternal."

Cristiano Ronaldo also sent his condolences to Brazil and Pelé's family in a post on Instagram, saying a mere "goodbye" to the eternal King Pelé. Kylian Mbappe said on Pelé's death, "The king of football has left us but his legacy will never be forgotten." Even the Brazilian President, Luiz Inácio Lula da Silva in a tweet said, "Few Brazilians took the name of our country as far as he did." He added, "As different from Portuguese as the language was, foreigners from the four corners of the planet soon found a way to pronounce the magic word 'Pelé'."

Pelé had always been open with his fans about his health. He admitted to undergo surgery in 1977 to remove his right kidney after he faced complications from a broken rib. He also had surgery to remove kidney stones. Once, after cancelling an event at the Pelé Museum in Santos, Brazil, due to abdominal pain, Pelé was diagnosed with kidney stones.

It wasn't all, in 2019, Pelé was again admitted to the hospital for a urinary tract infection and underwent another surgery to remove kidney stones. After the surgery, *Agencia Brasil* reported that "The procedure was successful and he is already in the room, in good general condition from the clinical point of view, according to his doctors." Thanking his fans, Pelé also tweeted, "Thank you for all your love! The antibiotics are working and the tests are all normal. I feel so much better, I think I'm ready to play again!"

Even after having so many complications and ups and downs in his life, Pelé never give up and he continued to be an inspiration for the world. Till his last breath, he was happy with his life. I am sure that he will be forever alive in our memories and serve as a role model to the coming generations.

❑

Pelé's Life Events

1940 Born on October 23 in Três Corações, Brazil. His parents named him Edson Arantes do Nascimento.

1946 The family moved to Bauru, Brazil.

1956 Joined the Santos club's junior team.

1957 Included in the top division team of the Santos club.

1958 Brazil became World Champion with the help of his two goals in the World Cup held in Sweden, and Pelé became world famous overnight.

1962 Brazil again won the World Cup Championship in Chile.

1966 Married Rosemari Cholbi. Participation in the World Cup held in England, where Brazil was defeated.

1969 Scored his historic 1000th goal.

1970 In Mexico, Brazil won the World Cup title for the third time under the leadership of Pelé.

1971 Announces retirement from international football competition.

1974 Retired from the Santos club. Refused to play in the World Cup.

1975 Agreed to come out of retirement and play for the New York Cosmos Club to popularize football in America.

1976 Led the Cosmos team.

1977 Led the Cosmos team and drew huge crowds in the North American Soccer League.

1977 Retired from football on October 1. Honoured by the United Nations as a World Citizen.

1977 Started working with UNICEF.

1978 Birth of daughter Jennifer.

1982 Separated from Rosemari.

1994 Second marriage with Assiria Lemos Seixas.

1995 Became the sports minister of Brazil.

1996 Birth of twins, son Joshua and daughter Celeste.

1999 The International Olympic Committee declared him the best athlete of the 20th century.

2000 Spent the decade playing the role of Goodwill Ambassador in the field of football from Brazil.

2008 Separated from second wife Assiria.

2012 Attended the closing ceremony of the London Summer Olympics.

2016 Third Marriage with Marcia Aoki.

2022 Died at the age of 82 on December 29.

❑

Important Quotes by Pelé

- Enthusiasm is everything. One can learn from it and it can be tightened like the strings of a guitar.
- I have accepted the fact that the life of a person running ahead is tough. He gets hurt more than others and the wounds he gets are not coincidental.
- Training is everything.
- Penalty is a cowardly way to score a goal.
- For twenty years they have been asking me only one question—who is the greatest, Maradona or Pelé? I tell them if they look at the facts, they will see how many goals he has scored with the help of his right foot or his head.
- Victory tastes sweeter when it is hard to win.
- Children all over the world who play football want to be Pelé. The biggest challenge before me is to set an example of an ideal player as well as an ideal human being.
- Wherever you go, people immediately recognize three names – Jesus Christ, Pelé and Coca Cola.

- I am often asked about the best players. I want to say that to win, it is necessary to play in favour of the team. Football is not meant to be played by one or two or three or four players.
- When a player scores a lot of goals, people start considering him as a great player. Goals are very important. But a great player plays a variety of roles on the field. He can help other players, encourage them, and motivate his teammates to move forward. He is someone who proves to be the leader of the team in bad times.
- I remember the World Cup matches of 1950 when I was 9 or 10 years old. My father was a football player and there was a huge celebration. But I saw my father cry when Brazil lost to Uruguay.
- I represent Brazil around the world. I want to display excellence wherever I go because I don't want to let the Brazilian people down.
- I have a philosophy of life, which I inherited from my father. He often used to say – Son, God has given you the talent to play football. It is a gift from God. If your health remains fine, then you will always remain vigorous and then no one will be able to stop you from moving forward with this gift from God. But you have to be fully ready.
- Brazil eats, drinks, and sleeps football. It lives football.
- There is no doubt that I am earning more from advertisements than what I used to earn while playing.
- I have been grateful to God all my life. My family has been a very religious family.
- I have always thought that if I had not become a sportsperson, I would have definitely become an actor.
- The World Cup is a very complex tournament – there are six matches – there are seven matches if you reach the final. You can be out of competition after losing even one match even if you are the best.

- Pelé cannot die, Pelé will never die. Pelé will live on.
- While dying, I will be satisfied that I have put my talent to good use. I have been able to achieve a lot through sports as it is the biggest sport in the world.
- Sports are a motivating tool for the young generation.
- Everything on earth is a game. Everything passes and eventually will die, we all have the same end.
- I don't think I'm a successful businessman. I take all decisions with my heart.
- If you don't educate people, they can be easily misled.
- Everyone knows about my life. I have won many tournaments and scored more than 1000 goals. I have won three World Cups, but I have not been able to play in the Olympics.
- I have to have faith in something that gives me strength. I have to believe something. But there were many moments in my life when I asked God for help.
- If you are the best, then you are the best. If you are in the second position, then you are nothing.
- Success is not a coincidence. It comes from hard work, patience, study, dedication, sacrifice and most important thing is how much you love your work.
- I don't believe in the concept of a born football player. You may be born with some talent and ability, but no one is born with training from their mother's womb.
- When football stars go down, teams go down with them and it's kind of an interesting phenomenon. It is like people coming to a theatre to see a great artist perform and if this great artist falls ill, the whole troupe has to bear the brunt.
- Freddy Adu plays brilliantly with the left foot, like Mozart's music.
- I think Romário will score 1000 goals, but he will not be able to break my record.

- ✦ Ronaldinho is the greatest player in the world right now. He is a player who has brought immense joy to the Brazilians.
- ✦ I sometimes wake up at night wondering why I'm still so popular. To be honest, even I don't know the reason for this.
- ✦ Messi is a great player. He is capable and intelligent.
- ✦ To become a striker, you need to be fit.
- ✦ The standard of football in England is high. English football can be called the leader of the world.
- ✦ When you are young, you do a lot of senseless things.
- ✦ Of course, my father was a great football player. When I was eight or nine years old, I wanted to be like my father.
- ✦ For years I have been living with two persons in my heart. The first is Edson, who hangs out with friends and family and the second is Pelé, a football player. I don't want fame.
- ✦ At the age of 17, I started to understand responsibility as I started taking care of my family. But I was young in football. I didn't have the experience, nor was I the captain—I was just part of the team.
- ✦ You should respect people and stay fit. I used to work hard. When all the players would go to the beach after their workout, I used to toss the ball at that time.
- ✦ When I retired, I got many offers to play in Europe, England, Italy, Spain, and Mexico. But I refused and said that after 18 years I want to rest, that's why I am taking retirement.
- ✦ Edson is the person who helps Pelé. Edson is the base. Pelé just comes and puts the face to him.
- ✦ At 16, I was playing for Santos and we had a great team. That helped me a lot. Then, I played for Brazil against Argentina in Maravasa. I got more experience. That was a year before the World Cup. These things had a great impact.
- ✦ It is not easy to execute a bicycle kick. I have scored 1283 goals, of which only two or three were scored in this way.

- I am proud that I was named Edson after Thomas Edison. I prefer to be called Edson. I find the name Pelé strange. Edson sounds like a serious and important name.
- When I was Brazil's sports minister, I tried to introduce a law that, like other businesses, would require the operators of football clubs to disclose their earnings. However, I could not succeed in doing so.
- Brazil has always had great players who have played at home and abroad, but we need to combine all the talents to create a great team.
- When you are playing against a bad player or a hot-tempered player, it can be easy to defend yourself since you can anticipate their moves. But if a hot-tempered player is also clever, then defence becomes difficult.
- I was not injured due to any attack in 1963. Still, I don't feel sorry because Brazil won. I had participated in two matches, that's why I was also given a medal.
- It is true that I am interested in business, but I do not work for everyone. I choose companies very carefully.
- I think it is difficult for a second Pelé to be born because my parents have turned off the machine. Great players will always be born. Some of those players may play more matches than Pelé or score more goals than Pelé. But I don't think that it would be easy.

❑

Glossary

- **Bicycle Kick:** The player tosses the ball backward over his head in the air. Often, he tosses the ball with his feet at chest height.
- **Corner Kick:** The kick is awarded to the attacking team when a player on the defending team kicks the ball near the goal line. A corner kick is executed from the corner of the field where the goal line meets the sideline.
- **Cross:** This is a kick that is executed from one end of the field to the other.
- **Dribbling:** Controlling and pushing the ball forward with the foot while running.
- **Forward:** The player on any team who is most responsible for scoring goals. These players always move forward and play and strive for the goal.
- **Free Kick:** This kick is awarded to the player in return for a mistake made by the opposing team. The players of the

opposing team must stand at a distance of 10 yards and they cannot move from their positions before the kick is executed.

- **Goalkeeper (Goalie):** A player who stands in front of the net to stop a goal and prevent the ball from entering the net. The goalkeeper is the only player allowed to handle the ball with his hands and arms.
- **Header:** Method of tossing the ball with the head.
- **Midfielder:** The player who plays in midfield and provides support to the forwards and fullbacks.
- **Penalty box:** This is a rectangular area in front of the goal. The goalkeeper can only handle the ball with his hand inside the penalty box. If there is a foul by the defending team inside the box, the attacking team is rewarded a penalty kick.
- **Penalty Kick:** When a penalty is scored inside the penalty box, a penalty kick is awarded as a reward. Only the goalkeeper can defend a penalty kick.
- **Save:** When the goalkeeper stops the ball from entering the net, it is called a 'save'.
- **Seleção:** The group of players from which the Brazilian national team is formed.
- **Tackle:** When during the game, a defender snatches the ball from another player without committing a foul.
- **Trap:** After intercepting the ball, it is controlled with the help of the body and the feet.

❑

Reference Books

1. *Pelé: My Life and the Beautiful Game* by Pelé with Robert L. Fish
2. *Pelé* by James Buckley Jr.
3. *Pelé: A Biography* by James Haskins
4. *Pelé* by Dax Riner
5. *Pelé: The Autobiography* by Pelé
6. *Man with a Mission: Pelé* by Larry Adler, Bruce Curtis, and Joe DiMaggio
7. *Pelé* by Francis the baud
8. *Pelé* by Rod Smith
9. *Learning Soccer with Pelé* by Pelé

❑❑❑